THE VICE PRESIDENT

THE WAR DIRECTIVE

When War Is the Only Option

Carolinadeivid

ISBN-13: 9781916439788
[Imprint: Touchladybirdlucky Studios]

A David Gomadza Production.

DEDICATION

"We have achieved great over the centuries. People have fought and died for us to have what we have today. The dreams of all those who died were to take humanity to the next level of advancement as nature intended. Unfortunately, some have forsaken all that and are taking us back to the time we had nothing. The time we were ravaged with all kinds of problems. We cannot let that happen! We have rights and obligations to preserve and advance humanity. Unfortunately, some have chosen the evil road, but I stand here today and declare war to them. We shall attack like a wildfire from all corners of the earth until there is not even a smoldering stump left."

DISCLAIMER

This is a work of fiction. Names, characters, businesses, places, events, and incidents are either the products of the author's imagination or used in a fictitious manner. Any resemblance to actual persons, living or dead, or actual events is purely coincidental.

ACKNOWLEDGMENTS

A big thanks to the Touchladybirdlucky Studios and best wish to the Carolinadeivid Brand.

UNDERLYING PRINCIPLES

Hostis Humani Generis:
"The torturer has become – like the pirate and the slave trader before him... *Hostis Humani Generis* an enemy of all mankind", wrote the court. *Filártiga v. Peña-Irala* *[Wikipedia]*

Jus Cogen: A peremptory norm...is a fundamental principle of the international law that is accepted by the international community of states as a norm from which no derogation is permitted." *[Wikipedia.]*

Universal Jurisdiction.
"...certain crimes pose so serious a threat to the international community as a whole that states have a logical and moral duty to prosecute an individual or state responsible; therefore, no place should be a safe haven for those who have committed genocide, crimes against humanity, extrajudicial executions, war crimes, torture....." [Wikipedia].

The only time the world got together [Collective justice] putting their differences aside to deliver justice and protect humanity from evil forever.

The Rise of Tomorrow's World Order: with a military wing and powers to execute justice swiftly and instantly stripping away individual and state immunity in a flash. No one is immune.

A house has a head

A school has a Headteacher

A university has a Chancellor

A military has a Commander-In-Chief

A country has a President/Prime Minister

For the first time in the history of mankind the Globe has a Global Leader: The rise of Tomorrow's World Order. [TWO] The current institutions are not fit for purpose and incapable of addressing global issues for most they are just extensions of the people who created them people also involved in secret-rights-abuse. TWO shall address all the shortfalls of these institutions: lack of a military wing, lack of power to strip away state immunity among others.

The rise of the Inbuilt-Gun.

The world should move away from defensive economies to proactive superior economies that foster human development and its advancement as the way nature intended.

CHAPTER ONE

"I think you are overreacting. None of the things you mentioned warranty such a global response."

Gabriel shook with rage unable to contain his anger. He got up and staggered toward the window in the office. He flipped the curtain sideways.

"*Hostis Humani Generis* if you ask me?"

Henry spat the wine out of his mouth.

"What?"

"You heard me!"

"No. Gabriel, anger can cloud your judgment. Why don't you take a break from all this? I will assign someone else."

"Why are you defending them? We all know that they have become worse than the pirates and the slave traders before them. In fact, they are still doing what was abolished years ago. I don't care whether it's done secretly or not that won't change the fact that they have become the enemies of mankind."

"Can you prove it?"

"You are missing the point. Are you familiar with the term; *Jus Cogens?*"

"Probably?"

"There is a universal agreement that torture, crimes against humanity, genocide, etc. are unacceptable. It's compelling law. These are values from which no exemption is permitted. Violations of these laws automatically makes one a *Hostis Humani Generis*. An enemy of mankind and as such thus any nation can capture and put him or her on trial."

"Saying it, is one thing and proving it is another."

"Henry, listen to me. Torture and other crimes like genocide are violations that are of global concerns. These are laws that were put in place to create a torture-free-world yet despite all these they are still derogating from these."

Henry walked to the window and looked outside.

"Let me tell you perhaps the oldest story you will doubtlessly hear."

Gabriel interrupted.

"There is no justification for evil doings whatsoever. These are peremptory values from which no derogation is permitted."

"Don't be too quick to judge. I am just saying put yourself in their shoes."

Gabriel glared at Henry with evil eyes.

"You are not getting what I am saying. I am saying there is no justification whatsoever to commit these crimes. None! These are near universal agreements that torture is unacceptable. Comprehend?"

Henry smiled.

"Hear me out first. The story goes like this. This bible Pharaoh accepted people from other countries but then realized that his way of life was inconsistent to what these people expected. He didn't want to change his ways, but he was not bothered by their presence only if they didn't interfere. The people grew cleverer and realized that universal norms and rights were being violated. They raised the issues, but this Pharaoh realized that he had to do something before things got out of hand. He ordered all midwives to unlawfully tag all kids born to foreigners. He ordered the midwives to kill all male babies in order to preserve his people. Killing according to him, would guarantee purity of his people's gene-pool. There can never be dilution of his people even if it means killing all these foreigners so be it. He suggested."

Gabriel paced in the office fuming with rage.

"Nevertheless, that is not a justification for derogating from peremptory values."

"Let me finish. See, he was in a predicament. He had a goal to preserve his culture. A duty to preserve his people by avoiding dilution of his people's genes. A duty to preserve and ensure the existence of his people. A duty to limit the foreigner's population so as not to grow to cause problems in the future. What can he do?"

Gabriel instantly stopped and gazed at Henry.

"Let me get this straight. You are suggesting that he has to kill members of the group?"

Henry looked at him and nodded.

"Further, he has to cause serious bodily and or mental harm to the group?"

"Precisely, so that no one can context his leadership in the future. Who will if they are all lunatics? See my point."

"Hang on, are you implying that this was a plan to preserve the gene-pool of his people thereby sustaining their existence?"

Henry smiled and sipped his wine.

"Don't tell me that you are suggesting that they are consciously creating conditions that will make it impossible to miscegenate? Does that mean that the use of these watermarks is true?"

"Listen Gabriel like I suggested he is doing everything to protect his way of life. His God given right. So how can you suggest the *Hostis Humani Generis?*"

"They are creating conditions to curb births of the group through use of man-made-viral agents and secretive threats."

Henry looked at him and smiled.

"Do you know how many foreign parents are declared unfit to look after their own kids? Do you know how many kids are in foster homes?"

Gabriel stopped and glanced at Henry.

"Wait, a minute."

Henry stared at him and smiled.

"Genocide."

"Damn it! All the elements you have mentioned are the exact points needed to successively argue a genocide case as defined in Article 2 of the Convention and Prevention of Genocide Act of 1948."

"The oldest trick in the bible."

"If it's so in the open why has no one contended that way."

Henry flashed his winning smile.

"It takes a great mind and great courage you know."

He paused.

"My friend the bible is the answer to all your problems but not the way everyone understands it today. You must go deeper. Nevertheless, the fact remains that one man's freedom fighter can be another man's terrorist."

"Article 1 of the 1984 Torture Convention refers to

torture *as a certain fundamental dominant principle of international law that can never be broken."*

"Gabriel the main question here is that can you prove it to warrant a global solution?"

"Proving it or not a *Hostis Humani Generis* is mankind's enemy and torture has universal jurisdiction and as such the world should be called upon to take action and deliver justice."

Henry beamed.

"Do you think that all these people don't know that? This is a plan implemented with the full knowledge and intent to cause all the points argued above like I said in order to preserve their way of life."

"Precisely the requirements for a genocide case to succeed."

"If you open the Bible, Exodus 1:15, it reads:

Then the king of Egypt told the Hebrew midwives, whose names were Shiphrah and Puah, 16 "When you help the Hebrew women in childbirth, look at the child when you deliver it. If it's a boy, kill it, but if it's a girl, let it live."

"Likewise, today's midwives have adopted the same roles especially with this technological advancement that has seen boys getting killed easily."

"What do you mean?" inferred Gabriel.

Henry smiled and walked to his comfortable sofa.

"There is a lot you don't know."

He put his hand in his pocket and took out a coin and flipped it in the air before tossing and twisting it. The coin spinned several times before it flattened on top of the table. He picked it up and showed it to Gabriel.

"In life there are two sides of everything would you agree?"

Gabriel looked at the coin and sat down.

"Sure."

"Just like a coin. Tossing it can give you two outcomes; a tail or a head, good or evil and a gift or a curse."

"So, what are you saying?"

"You know why no one believe people like you? It's not because you don't know what you are talking about. No. Neither is it that you are lying. No."

Henry supped up his wine.

"So, what is it?"

"It's simply because they are very clever, deceitful and very devious. They have created a technological tool that is claimed to help everyone. Most swear by it because to them this has been a life changing tool with goodness after goodness. But little do they know that even though the same tool is like a coin with two sides. To them every time they have tossed the coin, they have always got one outcome that is the tail and never the head side, but there are two sides of the coin. What do we know about the probability of tossing a coin?"

Gabriel sat up straight.

"Since the coin is fair, each flip has an equal chance."

"Precisely, but this is the trick. Their coin is jammed so that they can only have one-outcome. In other words, this is a controlled outcome. A programmed sequence. A pre-defined outcome. Whereas in situations you are talking about the outcome is left to chance. Any outcome good or evil has an equal chance. Having that in mind. All the people you have approached just for argument's sake have their coin stuck on one probability; the good side. They also know that you and they have the same tool so to them it's obvious the outcome for both you and them will always be good. This is because this is the only outcome they know. Mentioning otherwise is something that is remote and very impossible. You both are on the same footing so to them you might simply be talking another language."

"In one person the same tool is a blessing in that it helps a couple conceive as it is used in fertility treatment yet to the unlucky ones the same tool can be a curse that it actually prohibits conception. Therefore, acts like a fertility hindrance."

Gabriel got up.

"Genocide! Article 2d. *Imposing measures to limit and control population growth through controlling births.*"

Henry smiled.

"The same tool can be used to impact and or alter eggs, embryos and sperms etc. through continuous shaking and inducing reactions through electric stimulation and that can be easily done remotely."

"You mean causing baby deformities and miscarriages?"

"Absolutely, remember the Pharaoh's plan of trying to control the population by limiting the number of births and killing those already born.

Exodus 1.22:

Then Pharaoh commanded all his people to throw into the Nile every Hebrew boy that was born, but to let every girl live.

"This not only destroys the young boy babies but also controls population by deterring the people from having kids or wanting to have kids if rates of deformities and disabilities are high."

"Is that humanly? Genocide I would suggest?"

"Precisely, all points mentioned so far; genocidal attributes."

Henry smiled further.

"It does not end there."

Henry smiled and sipped his wine.

"Tell me about it. The tool itself cause unwanted outcomes to scare people and prohibit births. The problem is the ability to convince those you reported to that the same tool they have is the same tool that is causing all these defects in kids. The same tool that is increasing disability rates. Mind you to them this tool is a blessing. Like I have pointed out above. There are two sides to everything. On one hand the same tool helping a couple to conceive on the other the same tool causing infertility in another couple."

"Wait, a minute. The discriminatory aspect of genocide?"

"You got that right."

"Another fundamental requirement in order to successfully argue the genocide and crimes against humanity cases?"

"Precisely. The Pharaoh was afraid that his people were going to be diluted by these foreigners, so he devised this plan with full intend and knowing exactly what he was doing. Implemented these acts that in turn amounted to genocide as there was a discriminatory element toward the outsider."

"Like I suggested, saying it is one thing and proving it is another thing."

Gabriel gnashed.

"Now that you clarified some issues for me, I think I will be able to prove that all their actions amounts to genocide even though they have their own reasons."

"Just Cogens!"

"Exactly. No matter what their justifications might be.

to preserve their gene pool, their way of life, avoid dilution of their people etc. still in international law they are derogating and breaking these compelling law norms from which, no derogation is permitted with suffering the consequences."

Henry nodded his head.

"It boils down to how can you prove it otherwise it's an open-and-closed case. Guilty as fuck."

A brief knock at the door interrupted the two men. Henry's secretary opened the door and stood there.

"Can I bring in your coffee Sir?"

Henry raised his hand and instantly the woman left before the door was shut behind her.

Gabriel got up and walked to the cabinet.

"What about these epidemics which conspirators have attributed to man-made agents? Can we establish the nexus?"

Henry smiled and looked at Gabriel.

"The bible my friend has all the answers. What do you know about the plagues of Egypt?"

"God punished Pharaoh for disobeying him by not letting the Israelites go?"

"Okay for argument's sake let's just say there is no God."

"What? I grew up in a Christian family and I strongly believe in God. Behold. I am Gabriel; the archangel.

The messenger of God."

They both laughed.

"My friend what people don't know is that the bible is a colonizing tool or a manual."

"Henry is it the wine? Maybe you should have your tea."

Henry smiled.

"Wine calms me down but I am as sober as a war horse."

There was a moment of silence.

"The bible is like a coin as I have suggested at the beginning. It has two meanings. One to you and another to the others. The bible was written as a manual for colonizing and conquering the world."

Gabriel grinned.

"You think I am joking. That is what the people don't realize. The bible was written as a secret, concealed conquering manual with exact methods of how to conquer and remain in power."

Gabriel cursed.

"Henry stop drinking the wine my friend. Colonizing manual? I don't think so. The bible is a good book showing mankind how-to live-in peace."

"You seem to contradict yourself. A minute ago, you said that the tool was a bad thing being used to cause genocide."

"The same as the bible. To you, you only see one outcome, or you have the tail side of a coin no matter how many times you toss the coin. Why? They let you see only that side, and to you, I can't blame you because this is the only side you swear by? The only side you know."

Gabriel looked down and listened attentively.

"The plagues are ways of controlling the population assuming there is no God, and the bible is written by man as a manual of how to colonize and stay in power. First let me explain this. To reiterate I said the Pharaoh wanted to preserve his people by avoiding dilution through miscegenation and limiting the foreign population, right?"

"Right."

"To Pharaoh to preserve his population he must also find a way of preserving that population. Have you ever heard about watermarks?"

"Off course! Used to deter use of something or allows other to know the rightful owner of something,"

"The plagues are watermarks that can be used to preserve such a people and punish the others. All at God's disposal to use to punish Pharaoh. Today's man-made viral agents are used to preserve and limit births. Look at the convention, I quote:

"*Article 2 of the Convention and Prevention of Genocide*

part: 'deliberately inflicting on the group conditions of life calculated to bring about its physical destruction in whole or in part.' Imposing measures intended to prevent births within the group;

Henry stood up and sat on the corner of the table.

"First like I argued above the Pharaoh to preserve his people he had to come up with ideas that will only affect the foreigners and not his people. In this case the development of viral-like watermarks to preserve his people comes to mind and the manufacturer of antidotes so that they won't be affected. That means also no antidote to the foreigners. Having said that let's look at the plagues to get a better understanding; Plague 1. This was used to control population by way of changing or imposing conditions that would cause death and destruction of a population or group. Turning water into blood. Water can mean life and if life is turned into, blood could mean death,"

"Article 2-part c; 'deliberately inflicting on the group conditions of life calculated to bring about its physical destruction in whole or in part"

Henry paused and looked at Gabriel.

"Yes, the idea being that killing fish in the river will starve the people of food, destroying the water, making it stink thereby discouraging its consumption by the others,"

"Are you saying a genocide tool to limit and control birth?"

"You can say that. It boils down to the same idea. Do anything it takes to preserve the people's gene pool and way of life at any expense. Even if it means using man-made viral agents so be it."

"Plague 2. Creating nuisance deliberately by choosing people who will cause disturbances of peace. Send thieves to break in and steal and cause all kinds of issues to make their stay uncomfortable. This can mean toy-soldiers or kid soldiers."

He paused.

"Plague 3. Making and the use of man-made viral agents that can be used to cause all kinds of issues discouraging births and in turn limiting population growth. You can say a genocide tool also nevertheless a crime. I can go on talking about all the plagues but if you look deep, you will notice that these are tools used even today to control population and preserve a people. Even if these can't be categorized successful as acts of genocide."

Gabriel looked at Henry before a knock at the door interrupted the two.

"Sir are you sure you don't want a cup of tea?"

"Okay bring it we might as well have some."

"So, this is a clear-cut case of guilty?"

"As I see it yes. Easy to establish the nexus. The link between the acts and the accused. Look at Pharaoh he did not carry out the attack or killings himself but ordered the midwives to act upon his call. The question applies to the case of the midwives who agreed and carried out the act therefore guilty and since it's a direct command from top the Pharaoh was guilty as well. If the midwives had refused, then that would be a different story altogether but obeying the order established the nexus' requirement."

"They can argue that they did not possess the means to carry out the attack?"

"My friend the world has developed, and technological advancement has meant being tortured remotely with someone you don't know. The guilt burden is on the whole institution and the Pharaoh who gave the command. Look at the drones, they are operated remotely same as the torture devices proof that torture is happening secretly and concealed. What if the device can emit a high-voltage-current that is used to torture the person? Even though it is operated at grassroots level. Nevertheless, this only points to the devolution of power to local councils and therefore these guilty as fuck as their leader."

"This is how you proceed. You need to automatically establish a widespread and systematic attack on a group here foreigners that is based on a plan and a policy devised by the Pharaoh or whoever if in power to curb population and avoid the dilution of his people's gene pool through miscegenation by the Israelites, etc. Therefore, you need to meet all the conditions to establish a genocide case."

"That brings me to another point. So far, I have a single detailed case that is beyond doubt an abuse and a violation of the peremptory norms. How do I prove that even though I can prove this case nevertheless the attack was systematic and widespread?"

Henry looked at Gabriel before lifting a cup of tea.

"The idea in extermination, where there are mass killings is to prove that even though the tool this time killed one, when the plan was to kill many still it can amount to an extermination. You only need to prove that the same tool at same or similar given situation has killed many even though in your case it killed one maybe because there was a signal jammer nearby that affected its operations thereby limiting the number of causalities."

"Having said that I think you are right to raise the notion of *Hostis Humani Generis.*"

"That's what I am saying that it does not matter in the global eyes what are your reasons or your justifications for carrying out torture. You can't torture someone in order to preserve your way of life. The fact remains that in the eyes of the international law you are an enemy of mankind therefore there is a universal jurisdiction. They have become like a pirate an evil of mankind hence the idea of global punishment."

"Remember also I raised the notion of one man's freedom fighter being another man's terrorist?"

"I know but still in law there are notions referred to as the *Jus Cogens*. They have a near universal agreement or consensus that they are referred to as compelling laws and norms which there is no derogation that is accepted. In other words, there is nothing sovereign above these acts. Torture, oppression, genocide and crimes of aggression are above Pharaoh or anyone."

"Are you suggesting that any agreement that first violates these is void?"

"Precisely. Any arguments to protect oneself that first violates these e.g. the non-use of torture is therefore automatically void because the treaty interferes with the Peremptory norms."

"This brings home my point that therefore violating these peremptory laws is considered as *Hostis Humani Generis*. An act that violates human rights globally and therefore any punishment is a global collective one."

There was a moment of silence.

"By collective action are you suggesting that each, and every country should punish them?"

"Exactly. We all have a collective duty to punish them as they have broken global rules. In other words, they have abused the whole global justice system, and the punishment is collectively decided."

"They cannot plead ignorant or unaware of global peremptory laws. Everyone knows oppression was abolished. Everyone knows no torture is permitted no matter what. Whether secretly concealed or not. Everyone knows extermination is classed as a genocide act. Everyone knows genocide is a crime. It does not matter what are your reasons. It could be to preserve your people still this interferes with compelling laws. Still a crime and as far as I am concerned there is no one above the law."

"Are you suggesting ganging up on them?"

"I know it sound harsh, but they have tortured and are still doing it no matter how it's disguised. Look at the epidemics in recent years even though we can't prove it now I think it will be easy to establish the nexus relationship. It can be said that they have a vested interest and as such we can easily establish the nexus criteria. They are still milking these places therefore they have every reason to control and monitor whatever happens there, and that gives us all the reasons to bring the case against them."

Henry threw a quick glance at Gabriel.

"Can you prove that they have implanted the [IMD] tool in all that died? Can you prove the tool is the one used to cause these epidemics? Can you link the victims and them? Can you prove there is a plan or policy being followed? Can you establish that there is a discriminatory aspect to all this? They can simply acknowledge that yes this happened but in the past and they can't be held responsible for their father's mistakes?"

"My point is that this can be proved. I argue that they are guilty because they are still perpetuating the evil done even if this was in the past instead of amending their father's mistakes. Looking at the past epidemics there is strong evidence to suggest whatever killed all those people was a man-made threat. Is it also not irony that the people affected had asked for more funding?"

"You mean; why not have poison instead?"

"Precisely even though this is just a logical thinking."

"This does not end there. The tool is a secret Weapon of Mass Destruction. [WMD] to be exact a remotely operated evil weapon of mass destruction [ROEWMD]."

Henry breathed heavily.

"I just can't believe that you even suggested that everyone has this tool. Are you implying that everyone has a weapon of mass destruction?"

"You said that a coin has two sides and for some they will never see the other side or outcome. Same applies here."

Henry touched his lips.

"I see. In that case can you explain further."

Gabriel sat up straight and gazed at Henry.

"The device is a lethal-high-voltage emitting tool

devised to literally fry someone. It can explode. Theoretically, anything that has a voltage has the capabilities of exploding if too much is introduced. Do you agree?"

"Certain."

"If the tool is cheap and can easily be implanted into the body, it can be a weapon. This can be done on a massive scale. If the tool is used to control body functions e.g., body temperature operated remotely like a drone, then it can be used to kill too. Logic thinking. If the device can be used to induce the good functions surely, it's open to anyone to suggest that thus as such the device equally can be used to produce evil. Having said that, I read in the papers of someone who was fried to death. Although in the paper the causes were attributed to the effects of the sun, this person was fried so badly that his eyes looked like those of a fried fish and trust me no sun can do that."

"Don't tell me that you are suggesting that the tool caused this?"

"Might have malfunctioned or has been hacked by the enemies."

"Gabriel still that cannot explain epidemics."

"I am getting down to that. The tool is like a cassette or CD player. It relies on a cassette tape or a CD to function properly."

Gabriel paused and looked at Henry.

"Yes, go on."

"The tool is like a computer, that requires software to be loaded into from an external source...."

"Wait, a minute. You said the tool is like a cassette, a CD player now a computer Make up your mind."

"Yes, it is like all those and more. First it relies on an external source to function properly. Picture a human being needing food to exist. The tool relies on externally induced software that commands it to carry out functions remotely? The device is used to artificially produce electric impulses that are generated and sent to various parts and organs of the body giving commands to expand or contract or to secret body fluids, etc. In other words, the device takes over your normal neurological activities and nerve functions. This is the same as in Hijacking."

"I don't believe you."

"Take a pacemaker for example it sends electric commands in the form of impulses to make the heart contract thereby producing a heartbeat. It relies on external control and inbuilt commands to control body functions of the heart. Correct?"

"Yes."

"If the tool can be used to carry out the good bodily functions what stops it to carry out the evil functions? Instead of sending the electric impulses it can be used to stop or block the electric impulses. Two sides of the coin remember."

Henry instantly got up and walked toward the window.

"Imagine the power one will have if they can control the whole world that way? Talking about greedy people who would want to enslave the whole world just imagine how the tool would appeal to them."

"Immensely huge gains. I agree. But it's just hard to believe that a man-made device is the one killing all these people?"

"Systematic and widespread killings, with intent and full knowledge of the acts. A plan and policy to control population and the resources' usage. Enormous vested interests."

"Crimes against humanity and genocide."

"They have relationships or connections and unconditional interests in all the affected areas. They are still milking these areas and therefore it can be argued that they have a plan or policy regarding these affected areas. Therefore guilty."

"The tool is used in the blackmailing of the people. Also, in the secretly intimidating and threatening of the people."

"But you also mentioned carrying out oppression? How can you explain that?"

Gabriel sat comfortably in his sofa.

"Oppression still exist even in cases where the victim has access to food, accommodation and nice clothes because they still lack freedom as they are secretly threatened or forced secretly without any rights to family life or expressions. The fact that they have a tool being used and manipulated remotely at their expense means that they are still in oppression. Most of these did not give consent. They were abused by the doctors. Heavily sedated waking up like that. To make things worse, the whole system then tries to implement and legalize evil. I say we need a global solution. Everyone should be involved in the attacks. The world has a duty to do away with evil. It's not rocket science you know. No. It's common knowledge that torturing and extermination among others are peremptory laws never to be broken. Break these at your own peril."

Henry folded his arms and looked at Gabriel.

"In that case I think we have every right to call the others and see what they have to say then we can move on."

"A lot of people have died for lesser crimes. These are *Jus Cogens* laws that are never to be broken without any nation facing the consequences of such an act."

"I agree."

Gabriel walked toward the door. He opened the door and stepped outside and then stopped. He looked back in.

"Rumors has it that they slaughtered 500K women and children so that they pay their debt."

"What debt?"

"Undisclosed. To make things worse, they are harvesting digital-souls."

"Digital souls?"

"The main reason often cited for going to war in the first place. To collect digital souls of dead women and children which they use as cures for the old and sick. Have you heard about the idea of subjugating?"

"You mean enslaving someone else."

"Precisely. The old person in this case would enslave the child or the woman in other words subjugate the 'state of mind' say tiredness to the device of the dead or sleeping child giving energy and relentlessness to the old person who would otherwise be bed ridden."

Henry rubbed his hands together. He sighed and sat comfortably in his sofa. Gabriel slammed the door behind him and left.

CHAPTER TWO

The door instantly opened, and a man walked in very fast pushing the door wide open. Delaney closed the door and walked toward his sofa in his office. Brynn stood in the center and gazed at him.

"What do you think you are doing?"

"Calm down everything is under control."

"Under control? Do you know right now they are summoning everyone? Do you know what that means?"

"Don't panic I have everything sorted."

"Everything sorted? They have invoked the *Hostis Humani Generis clause.*"

Instantly Delaney stopped.

"Can they do that?"

"I don't know you tell me? What have you been up to?"

Delaney smiled cheekily and was about to walk to the cabinet when suddenly Brynn grabbed his hand.

"Listen to me you. If you did something wrong, you are going down on your own. I have neither part nor lot in this."

Delaney's face instantly changed. He opened his eyes very wide and looked at his hand which Brynn had grabbed. Instantly Brynn let go of the hand.

"Relax. What can they possible do? Take me to the Hague? Please!"

"I am just saying whatever it is. I don't want to be involved. My hands are clean."

Instantly Delaney retracted a knife from his waist belt and pushed Brynn before putting the knife under his chin lifting his head up.

"Relax. I told you fear only me. No one else."

Quickly he placed the knife back and straightened Brynn's suit jacket.

"Why nowadays no one fears me. You fear all these people, yet I control all these people. I have my people everywhere. You should fear me."

Brynn walked to the window and stood there looking outside. He walked back to the center of the office.

"I am not trying to be funny you know. But I don't want to be involved in all this. I have worked very hard to be where I am, and I can't let you take me down with you."

Instantly Delaney looked at him with piercing eyes.

"Don't be a coward! I said don't worry about petty things."

"I think you are very cocky. They don't invoke the *Hostis Humani Generis* unless they have strong grounds to believe that they can succeed."

"Enemy of mankind. Me?"

Delaney smiled.

"You think this is a joke? I have worked very hard and can't let you destroy everything I have built."

"I swear I will kill you myself if you don't stop talking like that."

"Hey. Don't threaten me. Okay."

"Or else what? What are you going to do?"

"I am just saying you don't know me too."

Delaney laughed mockingly.

"I know you with that little fear-tail between your legs all the time like a small dog."

"Just being nice to you. Otherwise with this *Hostis Humani Generis* accusation I can afford to fight you than fight the whole world."

Instantly Delaney froze fear-struck. For the first time he looked like he had seen a ghost.

"Fight me? But you know I did this for you. I gave you the money right."

"No, you did not. You paid your debt where you got

the money from, I don't care. I don't give a toss! That's a fact."

Delaney laughed and walked to the cabinet.

"Laughable. I told them something along those lines too. I told them that how I got the money was none of their business."

"No. You listen! You pathetic loser. You didn't do this for me. I will never rob anyone let alone kill women and children. You are on your own."

"We are in this together you just don't know it."

Brynn grabbed Delaney by the collar.

"Maybe I kill you myself. This *Hostis Humani Generis* means everyone attacking you. Every country on earth going to war with you. How are you going to survive that? You can't run anywhere. You are finished. It's only a matter of time."

"I am not scared. I have friends who will fight on my side."

"Friends? You think all these countries are your friends? Think again. Someone showed them who you really are. A devious and manipulating son of a bitch. Stealing, robbing and killing people for nothing. To make things worse, you oppressed others. I am a man of principles. I don't see divisions. My hands are clean. I worked very hard for what I have."

Delaney laughed sarcastically.

"There is a saying that birds of the same feather flock together. You are like my wing-man. I go down. You go down too."

Brynn punched Delaney very hard.

"Don't compare me to you. Why do you do that? I have never killed women and children in cold-blood. I have never robbed anyone."

"You bastard shut-up!" shouted Delaney.

"Do you think that anyone can just give me what I want if I asked. You accepted the money, didn't you? Even though you knew how we got it? Why raise the issue today?"

Brynn punched Delaney again.

"I never knew you are a genocidal maniac committing crimes against humanity in the name of population control. Exterminating people and harvesting organs. I will never do that."

"We are in together."

Brynn pulled out his gun and aimed instantly at him.

"Maybe take you out myself."

"Trying to cover up your tracks?"

"No doing you a favor. You rather have all your people attacked and killed? Better just you die?"

Instantly Delaney retrieved his knife and stabbed Brynn on the arm. A loud growling sound of a man in pain filled the office. The door instantly opened. A man stood at the door aiming a gun at Brynn. Delaney raised his hand, and the man left closing the door behind him.

"You let me down by not putting your faith and trust in me."

"You are finished. It's only a matter of time before they come for you. For the love of God spare your people. Kill yourself run whatever."

Delaney smiled cheekily.

"You never understood me. I play God and you are asking me to fear men? Are you fucking stupid Brynn?"

"They are going to attack from all corners of the earth. Where would you go?"

"Stand firm and fight. You just put your little tail between your legs like always. I fight my own wars. I know the money was good."

"You owed me money you had a duty to repay your debt so where you got the money from is no big deal but if I had known that that's how you got the money surely, I was going to refuse it."

"They have nothing."

"This time you are going down. What's with this harvesting thing?"

"What harvesting thing?"

"They say you are collecting human body parts

everywhere killing at will."

"Don't believe everything you hear."

"They are saying that you are killing as if you are God leaving trails everywhere."

Delaney stopped and looked down.

"Trails. Me? Hmm. Impossible."

"What?"

Brynn looked at him with wide-opened eyes.

"So, you are still doing it?"

"They degenerate the value of my people through miscegenation. I have a duty to carry on our forefather's legacy of preserving a pure and an undiluted gene pool. I don't want the stigma of having to fail when everyone's else has succeeded in preserve our way of life."

"The world is changing. Move with the times."

Delaney walked to the cabinet and poured whiskey before washing his mouth with it.

"Don't point your fingers at me. You have no idea what I am going through. You don't know anything. Honestly, I don't care. I provided a home for them the only thing I asked for was that they should not degenerate our gene pool. Is that asking much?"

"You mean you abused them?"

"No. There is no abuse at all. I have rights too you

know. I have a right to choose my way of life. I have a right to preserve my way of life. I have a right to preserve our gene pool. I gave them a house. I gave them a home. I provided food and shelter. All I asked was to be left alone. That's all. That's my God given right too. Something that is often overlooked nowadays."

"I read the documents. They accused you of secretly torturing them."

"Who can prove that?"

"They have a video showing evil-hacking and torture beyond doubt maybe the main reason why they have raised the *Hostis Humani Generis*."

Delaney stopped.

"What video?"

"That's not the point! Damn it! Are you torturing them?"

Delaney instantly pressed a button on the telecom system.

"Yes, Boss."

"Come here right now!"

"Delaney answer my question. Are you secretly torturing these people and enslaving them?"

The door instantly opened. Delaney's bodyguard entered swiftly.

"Yes Boss!"

"Damn it! Why can't you be proactive? Find that tape if it means killing everyone do so!"

Brynn looked at Delaney with talking eyes.

"Don't give me that look. I have a duty to carry out. You don't know what it's like. I must carry out our forefather's legacy. I swore and made an oath. I gave these people a home. But no, they want my women too. Above all they breed like rabbits. I can't just tolerate that. The best line of defense are your people your undiluted people. Once they start mixing our legacy is finished. It upsets me when my own rights are swept under the carpet."

"I understand you are using man-made agents as well to deter them from miscegenation."

"Listen! I am like every businessman. I am no different to all. I have a precious possession. I want to keep it and preserve it. Just like a business person. I buy a watermark and claim that this is mine. Touch at your peril."

"They are saying that you are using man-made viral agents as watermarks."

Delaney poured another glass of whiskey.

"Businessman thinking and attitude. I have valuables I find a way of securing them. In-case some steals them then he or she is in for a bargain. How do I know who stole my possession? I trace my watermark. Tara, I got you! Common business thinking. Not an abuse tool like they want everyone to believe. If I let them breed like rabbits how am I going to avoid one of them fighting to overthrow me tomorrow?"

"Their arguments are that you are using these man-made viral agents not just to deter but to instill conditions that will result in the death of the people, a genocide."

Delaney cursed.

"If you were in my shoes, you would understand. How can I preserve my people if I let them eat? I don't want their population growing. Tell me right now how I can manage that? You see what makes me angry is that people overlook the fact that I have given them everything on one condition; keep your dicks out of my people. Is that asking too much? I guess I have to fight."

Brynn sat down and lifted a glass of whiskey placed on the table by Delaney.

"My friend I just don't know what to do."

Delaney sat down too.

"Simple. Fight with me you are an accessory already."

Brynn looked shocked.

"Accessory why?"

"The money my friend. All those deaths you think that was a coincidence?"

Delaney laughed sarcastically.

Brynn's face fumed with raged he quickly tried to reach for his gun before crying in agony while looking at his bandaged hand.

"One day I will kill you myself."

The two men threw a quick glance at each other.

Arianna heard a man slightly coughing. She quickly got up and walked toward one of the houses in the compound. She entered the house and stealthily walked toward one of the rooms. She stopped and listened. Instantly she walked toward the room. She slid the door and a ray of light widened the more she pushed the door.

"Can I get you something?"

The man turned around and slightly opened his eyes.

"I said can I get anything?"

The man sat up straight on the bed.

"Sit down I want to talk to you."

Arianna sat on the chair next to the bed.

"How strange life can be sometimes."

"What happened?"

"It feels like yesterday when your father was our champion. Fighting to make us a people again and there you are."

Arianna looked at Kai a wrinkled old man so frail that you will think that he was about to die. She smiled for a while.

"I understand you knew grandpa too."

Kai breathed heavily. There was silence.

"How strange and sad that all would die so young."

"Just bad genes maybe or just unlucky."

Kai looked at Arianna and a tear dropped from one of his eyes. Shaking, he wiped his eyes.

"Have you taken your medicine are you in pain?"

Kai forced a smile.

"Pain? What do you know about pain?"

"I understand pain is unbearable."

"This pain I guess probably you will never experience it."

"What's wrong uncle you sound like you are dying. But unfortunately, all I see is a very healthy but lazy man who just want to sleep."

Kai shaking looked at Arianna and smiled before coughing slightly.

"Lazy me? I don't think so. I have no one to talk to. If you are not here, the bed is my friend. Maybe I should teach you the Stones-games. Maybe we play some days when I am feeling better."

"I never heard about the Stones-game before."

"Your uncle was very good at it and your father even better."

"If you were not in pain, I could have said let's go to the games hall and play for a while."

Kai looked down for a while.

"The pain I have is not pain for the flesh. No. It's pain of the soul."

"Uncle! What got into you today. Why are you scaring me?"

"I got your uncle killed. I got your daddy killed."

Arianna dropped the glass of water she was holding. She stood up speechless and stood there not knowing what to do.

"Even if I didn't pull the trigger, I choose money over them. What did I know then? For the first time money does not matter at all. Fear is crippling me. Dying before we are a people again."

Arianna sat down and listened attentively.

"I had a choice of saving both, but I chose money first. Nothing matters any more than our Torch being given back to us again."

"I understand you did your best. What more could you have done?"

"A lot."

There was silence.

"A lot. I could have fought to save them. My kids."

"I am sorry for your lose."

Kai started crying.

"That devious devil robbed me of all my kids one after the other. I betrayed your uncle and your father so that I can provide for my kids forever."

Arianna touched his shoulder.

"That devil should die. He offered us lifetime money with a lump sum every time someone pays for the Torch."

"So, are you saying that my uncle fund-raised money for the Torch and his father before him?"

Kay nodded.

Instantly Arianna got up and creased her face with rage.

"Oh no! I don't think so. Not me."

Arianna pulled a gun and pointed at Kai. In turn all he could do was to laugh.

"Who would I do this for? All my kids are dead,"

Arianna thought for a while before lowering the hand holding the gun.

"Back again I did it for my kids. All we did was not to show up."

"You let my uncle and father be ambushed?"

"It's not as easy as you think. For generations we have failed to get back the Torch. Your uncle and father were the only strong ones we had."

"What strong ones? Look where are they today?"

"They have become very clever and devious over the years."

"They should have acted like you. Think about us, your children."

Kai looked down for a while.

"They were actually clever otherwise you would not have been born."

"I thought yours died in accidents?"

"I thought so too but now I think they killed them."

"And left you alive?"

"I saved my kids and traded your father. Now I am too old with nothing. All that I own will go back to him. What could I have done differently? They say what goes around comes around."

There was a moment of silence.

"Promise me one thing."

Arianna looked at Kay.

"Promise me you will do whatever it takes and fight this evil and recover our Torch."

Arianna stood up and walked to the window.

"I don't want such a burden. Are you trying to get me killed like you did to my uncle and my father? No, I don't think so. I would rather shoot you in cold blood."

Kai smiled.

"I don't blame you. I can't be trusted. I have wronged generation after generation. But..."

Kai slightly coughed.

"But what?"

"There is something that can be done."

CHAPTER THREE

"Hostis Humani Generis! Hostis Humani Generis!"

The crowd shouted outside a huge government building.

"Jus Cogens! Jus Cogens! No one above the law!"

A man in a waist-coat flipped open the curtain and looked at the crowd.

"The world has gone mad. I guess enough is enough."

Brynn shrugged his shoulders.

"My hands are tied. That bastard set me up giving me stolen money. Surely I was going to join everyone."

"Enemy of mankind? I guess the world want change. A new beginning. Responsible leaders not some petty thieves killing thousands just to boost their egos. There is a new form of accountability. I guess no one is immune."

"Don't give me that look. What can I do? Accessory."

There was silence in the huge office and all they could hear was the shouting of the people outside.

"That bastard gave me stolen blood-money. I have the blood of innocent women and kids on my hands."

Hudson switch on the television.

"It's global. What else do you expect? You can't upset the whole world killing and robbing just to make strong strains of viral agents. I guess even his own people will turn against him. There is no disposable income in the economy people are suffering."

Brynn stood up and walked to the window.

"They are using starvation as a tool and a weapon to control the people. All these billions could have been better used to improve the life of his own at least he could have got some sympathy."

"It's nothing to do with looking after his people. The issues raised are that he has embarked on a large-scale plan to preserve the status quo at the expense of the people's universal rights hence the *Jus Cogens* claims."

"What can he do he made an oath to his father to carry on the legacy?"

"What the people are saying are that you can't preserve the status quo without infringing on the peremptory laws that have universal jurisdiction hence the *Hostis Humani Generis* claims."

"It seems true. I blame him. He should have denied these people in the first place. Why take all these foreigners when you don't want miscegenation to take place? Can't you see that something is wrong there?"

"There is no justification for torture or extermination of the foreigners."

"What are the others saying about all this?"

Hudson sat down.

"I have never seen such a thing. Everyone has a grievance. It seemed the people suffered in silence for years it seemed the lid has been lifted and everyone wants revenge. We have the Torch-people demanding that their Torch be brought back among others."

"What really happened with this Torch?"

"Some people hang-on to nothing. The Torch to them seems it has some magical powers. To them it defines them. It gives them the courage to go on. It reminds them of all those who died for them."

"What I don't understand is that why can't he just give back the damn Torch. He will risk getting all these people killed for that useless Torch."

"Control my friend. Control, with the Torch he can use them to raise money for him. He can tell them what to do. Just imagine the power you will have if you strip away what people believe in. You can control them."

"I think he is playing with fire. Who else has grievances?"

Instantly there was a quick loud knock at the door.

The door swung wide open. A man in military uniform appeared at the door.

"She said that it's important."

"Okay let her in."

The man instantly marched out before an instant knock startled both. Liliana, a smartly dressed a young woman walked in fast.

"Results inconclusive. No trace at all. Clean than suggested. Although the way they died resembled the test subjects."

The two men looked at each other.

"What are you saying?"

Liliana removed her reading glasses and looked at the two men.

"There is no way he could have used biological weapons. There is no way this was extermination as being argued. No traces or evidence of pathogen activity."

Brynn flipped the folder in his hand.

"This contradicts the findings from the project he commissioned as soon as there was an outbreak."

Hudson looked confused.

"I don't get it. The whole world is accusing him of being an enemy of mankind because he is using viral-agents to kill and rob. And then he sends in his own team to investigate. After that then his own team admit the people died of biological activity and you are saying that there is no biological activity, what are we missing?"

"I understand that after the outbreak he did send his special team., Right?"

"Right. If they are already dead why introduce biologicals after they are already dead?"

"Spread terror and fear."

"For what purpose?"

"The reports stated that biologicals were identified on all collected tissue. Right? But your finding states that there was no activity or traces of biologicals. What is he covering up? Definitely it must be bigger than the risk of being accused of extermination charges."

"What can be bigger than genocide charges?"

"When the people die. He sends in his teams and in all incidents his teams are first at the scene. They collect the tissue for testing. They declare presence of biologicals. They then leave with parts to investigate."

A sharp loud knock at the door interrupted the flow of thinking. Instantly the door opened, and a white glove held the door before a military man stood at the door.

"He said that it's important."

Hudson looked at Brynn and then at Liliana.

"Who is he? Are you expecting anyone?"

A man with long hair and beard dressed up scruffy entered the office. He pushed backward the locks of hair covering his face and smiled.

"Sorry to interrupt Mr. President but I have the answers. I want you to nail this devious son of a bitch. For decades he terrorized our people. He is smart no doubt about that. I guess that even if you have figured it out yourselves still you would not prove how he did."

"Go on we are listening."

"$100 billion?"

The two men quickly glanced at each other before they all looked at Liliana.

"You are performing a national service therefore voluntary and unpaid."

"Unpaid for serving humanity. Just imagine the credit you will get for saving women and children destined to die if the war breaks out?"

"The President is ordering you to explain."

Instantly his face shone with enthusiasm.

"You are all correct, but he thought he is clever. He is killing worldwide and harvesting?"

They all looked at him.

"Harvesting what? What can he possibly do with people who died that way?"

"I will quote from *Exodus 7:17-18 King James Version*

(KJV):

17 Thus saith the Lord, in this thou shalt know that I am the Lord: behold, I will smite with the rod that is in mine hand upon the waters which are in the river, and they shall be turned to blood. 18 And the fish that is in the river shall die, and the river shall stink; and the Egyptians shall loathe to drink of the water of the river.

"Son what is this? You think it is time to play games? What is this?"

"It's a power game. The rod in the hand here might refer to something operated remotely. The waters can mean the waves. Transmitting waves that kill the weak usually symbolized by water. Turning life into blood could mean death. All he is doing is altering through remotely operated killing-waves so that no one would associate with them sending fear and panic. But note also that whereas everyone else if afraid his people are not afraid. Why?"

"They know the reason behind this. To spread fear and panic turn attention away from the fact that he is an organ hungry maniac."

"Not just that but to monopolize so that no one else touch. He is an organ dealer. That explanation answers all your doubts and questions. First how come his team find and declare presence of biologicals when your own team find the tissue free from any impurities or agents? Secondly, he does this so that no one suspect he is an organ dealer otherwise he faces crimes against humanity and genocide. It makes sense, who cares about contaminated-tissue organs? No one. So, all his teams are first to arrive. To harvest whilst still fresh. They take organs for testing. But, not for testing but harvesting in broad daylight and on national television."

"Son of a bitch!"

"That can be used to explain genocidal claims too. Extermination at unprecedented levels."

"Do you mean to say that he is grooming all these people like chickens in order to harvest organs in the end?"

"Unquestionably."

A limousine parked outside a huge tall building and a young gentleman got out smartly dressed and instantly started walking very fast toward the building. A huge applause and people cheering made him secretly smile. The cheers became louder and louder as he walked away from the crowd that was outside, and with every step he made, the buzz grew louder and louder until a point he just stopped and turned around. He raised his hand. Loud cheers filled the atmosphere. He felt goosebumps. He looked from left to right and saw something he had never witnessed before.

"Sir, they are waiting."

David stood there for a while before waving and going inside. His heartbeat elevated, and his heart pounded with every step he made. He knew this was it. Time has come. It was like a divine calling. Ever since his childhood he had felt that he had a divine calling. He was destined to change the world as we know it today. He believed life could be better for everyone, regardless. He stood behind the huge doors. He could hear the roars inside and the huge buzzes. He could picture angry faces, he could hear hoarse voices, he could visualize discontent among everyone. Above all he knew he had a tough challenge. Humanity had known this life for the past 2000 years. The people's hearts were hardened. These people always fought for what they believed in. These people had done this for all their lives and have invested in these institutions. Who was he? Coming from nowhere and trying to change the norm. Many had perished just for thinking about it let alone fight established evil cults. It must start with someone. He thought for a while. It might be unthinkable today, but tomorrow people might realize its usefulness. The huge doors abruptly opened. He looked in front of him. The hall was filled with all the powerful men and women of the society. All global leaders and people of influence. He breathed heavily and walked first shaking but instantly he heard the roars and cheering of the crowd outside. He stopped and cheekily smiled. Instantly he clenched his hands holding his portfolio tight.

"Ladies and gentlemen thank you for coming at such short notice. The world is changing. Each year things are changing. Every century our needs are changing. Our priorities are changing too. Our tastes and way of life is changing too but…"

He stopped and looked at everyone.

"Our thinking is not changing neither is it adjusting to the problems we are facing today."

"Tell us something new!" shouted someone from a corner.

He stopped and looked around.

"Mankind has done a great job of putting laws in place to safeguard the existence of humanity and to deter evil practices yet even today we have countries and leaders still breaking these laws."

He paused and glanced at everyone.

"Ladies and gentlemen these laws are not just laws. They are special laws. Laws that have universal jurisdiction. Laws that everyone knows about. Laws fundamental to the whole fabric of the legal and justice system. Laws which breaking them not only make each country be held accountable but laws that have a global jurisdiction. Laws that are called the *Jus Cogens*, meaning that these laws are peremptory laws that no derogation are permitted. Those who are breaking these laws are automatically *Hostis Humani Generis.*"

He stopped and gazed at everyone. Everyone was silent and listening attentively. There was not even a cough heard.

"Yes, ladies and gentlemen. Hostis Humani Generis is an evil person, so evil that he or she is automatically considered as the enemy of mankind. Someone who can be attacked by the whole international community without any redress, someone who deserve the collective judgment."

A huge buzz filled the hall.

"Yes, ladies and gentlemen. I know it sounds so inhumane that a violator must be treated like this, but I think what should shock you more today is to know that today these *Jus Cogens* laws are still being broken and more often in broad daylight?"

A huge buzz filled the hall.

"Despite huge efforts to eradicate torture as an evil thing. We still have countries and institutions still torturing others although secretly but still torture is torture."

"That's bullshit!" shouted someone.

The usher pointed his hand in the far corner. A man stood up and looked at David.

"Tell me! If I must protect my interests how would I get the information I need? Some people deserve to be tortured to correct behavior. Dogs can be tortured to behave properly. Isn't that correct?"

The man did not expect an answer but instead proceeded.

"What can be a torture act to you, might be a good method to achieve results."

The people gathered spoke among themselves.

"Honorable ladies and gentlemen, we have come a long way. Our forefathers and all past leaders sat down and discussed these issues. After much consultations they then decided to pass the *Jus Cogens* laws."

He paused.

"These laws are fundamental laws. Laws in which there is no derogation whatsoever that is permitted. Any agreement or treaty that violates these is therefore automatically void."

There was a huge buzz.

David straightened his suit jacket and looked at everyone. Instantly there was instant silence.

"These laws include the following, but the list is not exhaustive; prohibition of the use of force, prohibition of oppression, prohibition of torture, and genocide among others. Having said that, the main problem we have today is not a lack of knowledge. No. Everyone knows, and everyone is aware that these laws exist. They are, I quote superior laws, superior norms sanctioning fundamental values' universally."

There was another huge buzz. People started shouting.

"Don't waste our time. We have institutions there already to address these issues. We have the Global Nations, we have the Global court, we have the Global criminal court."

David smiled and looked at the usher who instantly pointed at another person.

"We created these institutions to address these problems."

David nodded and smiled and looked at the usher who in-turn selected someone else to speak as well.

"We are punishing all the violators. We have judges whom we have put in place as well. What do you say to that?"

David nodded his head before putting on a seriously face as everyone stared at him. Instantly there was total silence. There was not even a cough or a sneeze.

"Ladies and gentlemen what if I tell you that you are the worst violators of these laws than the people you are dragging into these courts day after day?"

He put on a serious face and looked at everyone with piercing eyes. A huge buzz filled the hall. Some stood up and were about to leave.

"This is bullshit! We, the greatest abusers? You must be nuts? I have never been dragged to the Hague so how come you say that?"

"Sit-down Please!" shouted David. His face instantly creased with rage. His voice revealed some anger patterns as he spoke.

"Listen! It's mankind's stupidity to think that these evil cults are addressing the issues I have raised."

"Why not? We have established these institutions so that we tackle these issues and you think you can stand in front of us and chat bullshit?"

"It's humanity's stupidity to think that they can establish these institutions and solve today's global problems."

"Why not? You foul-mouthed power-hungry maniac!"

"Mind your language when you address everyone here."

"Or else what?"

"Ladies and gentlemen, it's inferior thinking and deceptive to all that you have establishing these institutions to solve today's issues."

"Why not? You know what? I am not going to sit here and hear you insult us. I am going." Timothy stood up and started walking out.

"Stop!" shouted David.

"Please sit down we need you. Personally, I would rather have you sat on your seat alive than dead somewhere else."

Instantly Timothy stopped, and everyone looked at David.

"Who do you think you are talking to me like that? I am a leader, the President of my country a sovereign nation. How dare! You, talk to me like that."

"Sit-down. Please."

"Who does he think he is?" shouted the people in the background.

"You are all violators of the *Jus Cogens* laws. You are manipulating and devious. Some of you exterminating thousands, dealing in illegal body organs harvesting and trafficking, most of you use secret torture, using advanced Remotely Operated Evil Medical Devices that are now formerly classed as Weapons of Mass Destruction, thereby making you answerable to me."

"Who the fuck are you?"

David walked closer to them.

"Your new global leader. The leader of leaders. The President of all Presidents."

"Who need that? I am a leader of my country that should be enough to me."

The people started talking. David stood there at attention like a soldier looking at everyone.

"Sorry mate but we don't need another leader."

Everyone started laughing.

David looked at his watch.

"You think this is a funny? You think this is a joke? Who said that?" asked David with a deep voice.

Finn stood up.

"You brat. I command a military. Try to disrespect me and I will get you shot in broad daylight."

"But I make you dance first. I reiterate. You are all guilty of genocidal crimes. Please sit down!"

Finn fumed with rage and took out his cellphone.

David looked at everyone and then at his watch before looking at Finn. In turn Finn looked at David and then punched a number before looking back at David.

Instantly as if in slow motion he lifted the hand holding the cellphone. David looked down at his watch and then at Finn before pressing the buttons. Instantly Finn dropped the cellphone to the ground and looked at his chest. Those around him heard the pops up as if buttons of his clothes were snapping. Everyone looked at him. His chest was expanding. His suit jacket tearing around joints. Beads of sweat droplets formed on his forehead before they rolled down.

"I said you are all guilty!"

"My chest! I am hot! I can't breathe!"

The surrounding people desperately removed his torn jacket and shirt. His body had suddenly become transparent. His flesh due to the expansion has become transparent. You could see his heart beating and enlarging at the same time. The vibrations of his heart were so pronounced that his body shook.

"Oh my God! Are you trying to kill him? Oh my God I can see through inside him! He is going to explode? He is going to explode."

"Stop it! Stop it! Okay, we will listen. Let him live!"

David twisted his watch and instantly Finn deflated before slumping back in his chair.

"You are just like everyone else then, evil. Bloody double standards."

"We all know your tricks." said David looking at everyone.

"You are a monster too!" shouted a lady.

"Hear me out ladies and gentlemen. The current system is inadequate to deal with global issues. Issues I have raised above."

"This is bullshit! We have established these institutions to deal with these problems. So please don't waste our time."

"Don't make me repeat myself!"

"Or else what? Torture us like you did to Finn?"

There was instant silence.

"This is a democracy. There is free speech. Finn brought that on himself."

"I suggest you become the leader of all these institutions we have already established if you are that desperate for power."

David looked at everyone.

"That's mankind's stupidity. You think you can establish an institution that will solve these problems? Do you think these institutions are solving the problems?"

"Yes. Why not? We have people being tried every time and sentences being passed."

"Bullshit! These institutions are there to cover your backs."

There was a huge buzz.

"It's like mankind creating 'gods' made of clay. The work of his own hands and then worship these as superior gods. It's the same principle."

"What the fuck is he talking about?" shouted the others.

"Ladies and gentlemen, I say abandon your inferior thinking. Okay let me put this in layman's terms. Everything on earth follows a set of rules. Do you agree with me?" shouted David his voice raising with every question he asked.

"Everyone needs a leader? Do you agree everything has leader? A house has a head. A school has a head. Do you agree?"

"Yes!" replied some while some grumbled.

"Every university has a Chancellor? Do you agree?"

"Yes!"

"All military has a Commander-in-Chief?"

"Yes?"

"Do you agree that every city has a Mayor?"

"Yes!"

"Every country has a President?"

"Yes!"

"So why the globe, the whole international community has no leader?"

"That's why we created these institutions to represent us globally you moron!"

"I said don't make me repeat myself. Capsci? These

institutions are the work of your hands. Therefore inferior! You surely are not telling me that if you break the *Jus Cogens* laws today these institutions are going to punish you for that? Are you?"

"Why not?"

"Simply because you created these. It was your ideas. Therefore, these institutions are to serve your purposes nothing else. Correct? These institutions are the work of your hands. They rely on your funding to function properly. Correct? So, in that case they are biased. Would you agree?"

A huge buzz filled the whole hall.

"It's fair ladies and gentlemen to say that these evil cults are there just to serve and maintain your existence. To defend you and sweep all your crimes under the carpet yet drag all the powerless and at times the evil leaders to Hague. But all in all, they are nothing than your extensions, other ways to devolve your power and spread your influences. These institutions are filled with your people. People loyal to you. People who would lick your ass. Correct."

"I can't stand this guy. Trying to destroy our way of life. Who does he think he is?"

"Ladies and gentlemen! Today I propose something bigger. Today I propose a new stage in human development. I say today's leaders are taking us back to the medieval times. Times when biologicals ravaged mankind. Times when threats were real. Times when they were concerned about was self-defense. I say this is inferior thinking. I say this is backtracking and as such is an inferior state of thinking. Let's move away from defensive governments and establish a new era. A new world order. A new way of thinking when defense is of less importance. I say let's start a new chapter when we are all proactive. When we foster human development. These institutions are powerless. They are the work of our hands and therefore not fit for purpose for they are simply an extension of yourselves. If you are corrupt, they too are. Simply because you made them. You put your people there. You wrote these rules. Rules which covers your back. Rules that gives you an alibi at the expense of the innocent. Where is the justice when 500K women and children not only die but their resources are looted as well so that the powerful can repay their debt? Are you telling me that these institutions will bring these perpetrators to justice? I say these institutions are biased. There to defend the most-evil. Those who created them. If one dies in their world, the whole country stands still. Where is justice there? This is not a case of abuse as the weak would want to jump to conclusion. This is a case about global injustice and the lack of effective structures to deal with the worst atrocities. This is about superior thinking. Like I said you can't make something with your own hands and worship that as your god. Likewise, you can't establish these institutions and tell me that they will protect the *Jus Cogens* laws. But...."

He stopped and wiped sweat now dripping down his neck. He unfastened his tie. There was complete silence.

"But ask Mr. Finn he will tell you that I meant business."

Everyone looked at Mr. Finn who was still clutching his heart.

"Yes. Mr. Finn will tell you that despite a thousand men under his command I nearly choked him to death without touching him. I would like to believe that this is the first time this has happened to him since the last time his mum slapped his backside."

David walked toward Mr. Finn and winked at him.

"I apologize I didn't mean to humiliate you but just to prove a point that..."

He walked toward the front of the hall.

"Yes, ladies and gentlemen. These institutions are the works of your hands. Surely a big brain will never worship a statue you made yourself. These institutions are just there to serve you. To foster and guarantee your existence. To make you feel that you are doing something about today's issues when in fact it's you the biggest culprits. You are the real *Hostis Humani Generis*. You are the real enemies of mankind. Using torture secretly to torture and imprison people without real grounds. You are the same people exterminating others. Breaking the *Jus Cogens* laws.

You are the same people still practicing oppression in the name of protection. But today this will end....”

He clenched his fits.

“Yes! Today we are going to set the record straight. Ladies and gentlemen for the past 2000 years what we have done is adopted, adapt then adopt again these defensive strategies. We spend more on weapons than on human development. It is you too, the same people effectively collecting resources everywhere leaving people without disposable incomes so that you make weapons. Yes, ladies and gentlemen starving your own people so that you make the strongest strains of viral-agents. Yes, the same people starving your own people so that you make the biggest missiles. The most destructive nuclear weapons. Yes, the same people robbing the poor. The soldiers who fought your stupid wars are starving? I know you are going to say these are local issues, but I tell you this. Change your thinking. Move away from defensive thinking. Let not fear of being attacked be your sole existence. I say foster human development and advancement the way nature intended. If a family of two became three. Does the head of the house look for a strong strain to kill the other member? Or ladies and gentlemen the head will always look for a bigger paycheck, a bigger house, etc. If you win the national lottery today do you build the most destructive weapon? Or you buy your family a new house or a new car? I know most will say here we go again here comes the socialist? But this is a superior human thinking attribute. All these institutions can never equal or replace what I am proposing."

He stopped and gave most a quick glance.

"Today I can say with much confidence that the whole system cannot solve real global issues. In order to address global issues, we need a global leader. Yes, a global leader ladies and gentlemen."

A huge buzz filled the whole hall.

"No. We have the UN we have all these institutions to deal with these issues."

David lifted his hand until there was silence.

"What I am proposing is a power great than all of you leaders put together. A power that can punish any country or leader who violates the *Jus Cogens* laws."

The crowd went berserk.

"Duplication! You are just a power-mad man."

"Ladies and gentlemen this is more than all these institutions. A powerful leader. The leader of all leaders. The President of all Presidents. I know probably you might have never heard this term, before; *Hostis Humanis Generis*. It's like a stubborn person so arrogant and devious that he is untouchable or thinks as such. This person is not just a criminal but an evil person so bad that there is universal consensus that he has done evil not just to the victims but to all mankind. We all have responsibilities, and we are all obliged by the laws of the *Jus Cogens* to act. Everyone is obliged to use force to bring this evil down. If it means the whole world collectively attacking this person so be it until there was not even a smoldering stump left. We are all compelled by the *Jus Cogens* laws to protect humanity. We all have duties to make sure no one on earth shall be subjected to torture. That no one shall be ill-treated. That no group of people shall be experimented on. That no group of people shall be exterminated so that their organs be harvested. ..."

There was complete silence. He walked from one corner to the other.

"These laws were developed over careful thought. These laws prevent and deter everyone to be good people, yet some have used technology to make Remotely Operated Evil Implanted Medical devices [ROEIMD] which they are using concealed deep in flesh without the person's knowledge to torture at will remotely. These ROEIMDs are worse than weapons of mass destruction [WMD] in that they are small nuclear, or radiation bombs remotely operated which produce radiation at the same time emitting a high-lethal-voltage current. A person who does this to another human being is the *Hostis Humani Generis* especially if he or she is doing it to self-gain disadvantageously at the expense of the victim. Exterminating people in order to control the population. Exterminating people in order to harvest organs. Exterminating in order to preserve his or her people. All these are *Jus Cogens* laws' violations. How can we deal with a *Hostis Humani Generis?* Who will identify, and look at the case and say yes, we have a case, and this is the way to move forward? The international court? The UN? Don't forget these institutions are created and are funded by people who fit the *Hostis Humani Generis* criteria killing in thousands and if not millions. I ask you a question today? Who is the target of your bio-weapon program? You are spending $ billions developing these and who is the target? Who are you going to experiment on? Are we expecting aliens from another planet? Without even answering this question you can see that the *Jus Cogens* laws have already been violated. The moment you wrote a check in tune of $millions to fund these activities the *Jus Cogens* laws have already made that act void and therefore you are automatically guilty and therefore an instant *Hostis Humani Generis.* An enemy of the people and therefore someone who deserves to be collectively attacked by all countries until you and your people are dead."

The people whispered among themselves.

"Ladies and gentlemen, I therefore propose and announce the establishment of a global power force with the power to bring any *Hostis Humani Generis* swiftly to account. A global force with a military and universal powers. Ladies and gentlemen, I introduce you to your Global President {myself} Mr. David the leader of Tomorrow's World Order. The leader of all leaders. The President of all Presidents. Let's move away from inferior thinking and let's make it a mandate to foster superior thinking while protecting everyone's rights."

There was a huge buzz and instantly the crowd from outside crashed the meeting entering the hall uninvited in numbers. The windows vibrated, and the ground shook as people outside celebrated and cheered.

"Justice at last! Justice for all! A better world! A new beginning! Let's bring evil down and hold everyone accountable! *Hostis Humani Generis*. Time is up! Justice coming to knock you down! Tomorrow's World Order! TWO- victory! Justice for all! A better world today! TWO victory!

The security guards rushed to restrain the people getting closer to the global leaders.

"To hell with this man! I will never be under you to hell with this Tomorrow's World Order! I am a President of my own country why do I have to be answerable to you?" shouted Dean.

Instantly there was silence.

David looked at everyone.

"Fair enough. I will sign your death certificate!"

CHAPTER FOUR

Delaney got up and walked to the window. He admired the view outside. Instantly a loud knock at the door distracted him. Instantly the door open and Kristy stood at the door.

"Sir."

Delaney instantly left heading to the study room.

He heard a huge buzz before opening the door to the huge meeting room. Instantly as the door swung open, there was complete silence.

"Ladies and gentlemen."

They all sat down as soon as he had sited down.

"It's not looking good."

Delaney raised his hand.

"But Sir..."

Delaney got up.

"I have to do whatever it takes to maintain our way of life. It's our God given right. It's my duty to carry on our way of living."

"But Sir it seems the whole world is slowly joining in the condemnation."

"Who cares? We have a duty to do and I expect you to do your part as well."

There was instant silence.

"Do you think we would be here if we listened every time someone criticized us?"

"The tide it seemed has turned."

"What do you mean?"

There was complete silence.

The men and women looked at each other first.

"The institutions have joined in as well."

"What? That can't be right. Are you sure about this?"

Delaney looked shocked but not shaken. He walked to the window and looked outside first.

"Sadly, it seems so."

"But it was my idea. I created these institutions. They are answerable to me. I do fund these bastards how can they do this to me? Put Audrey on the phone right now." shouted Delaney fuming with rage.

He paced left and right and stopped to talk over the phone.

"What am I paying you for?"

"But Sir..."

"Don't give me buts. Pass the ball. You know the drill."

"I am afraid I can't Sir?"

"What do you mean you can't?" shouted Delaney. There was complete silence. The stronghold of ten in the meeting hall with Delaney just looked at each other.

"We had no clue. He has gone global."

"I don't care."

Audrey sighed and waited for Delaney to give her the turn to speak.

"It seemed the world is ganging up on you Sir."

Delaney slammed the receiver down.

"Listen to me very carefully. I have a people to preserve and I want every men and women here to stand by me."

The men and women looked at each other.

"But Sir there is little we can do?"

Delaney slammed the table.

"Don't give that? I don't want excuses. OK?"

The men and women looked at each other.

"I have worked very hard establishing these institutions. All the people there are all answerable to me. So how on earth are you saying that they can't do what I want?"

"They have filed the Hostis Humanis Generis case."

Delaney looked shocked and scared for a split second.

"Hostis Humani Generis me? I thought that they were just rumors."

There was complete silence. He looked at each person in that meeting hall. The look on his face said it all. They all looked like they had seen a ghost. He could see a sense of helplessness and fear on all their faces.

"Don't tell me that you agree with these lunatics?"

He looked at everyone.

"Come on people. Tell me that you don't believe this bullshit... Do you?"

Rex stood up and breathed heavily.

"It's not that Sir."

He paused and looked at everyone else.

"They have compelling arguments and I am just saying it will be hard to prove otherwise."

"Damn it! Rex! Don't tell me you believe this bullshit. What about our ideology? What about what we stand for? What about our dreams? To preserve our people. Our ideology of creating a superior people. A people not ravaged by impurities. A pure people not riddled by disease, disability, deformities and all social evils. This is eugenics at its best. There is nothing wrong in eliminating the defects and unwanted social and biological traits. We have rights too just like them to choose what we want and how we want to live. Our values comes first. To us their queries are the very things we are fighting to eliminate. Surely don't tell me you believe this bullshit. Rex you of all the people surely don't tell me you lost hope too."

There was a moment of silence.

"All we are doing is believing in selective breeding. Improving the genetic composition of our people. This has nothing to do with them. Damn it! People! What about our rights? There is not even a single thread of truth in what they are saying. I believe just like my father and his father before him that diluting special genes with inferior genes will lead to the degeneration of our gene-pool. Surely you should agree with me?"

"It's not that we don't agree..."

"So, what is it? Tell me!" shouted Delaney.

The men and women looked at each other.

"They have strong grounds."

"Bullshit! Why are you saying that we can't safeguard and improve our people? What stops us eliminating the undesired features and encourage the desirable features. What is wrong in eliminating the imbeciles? What is wrong in eliminating disability? What is wrong in eliminating defective genes?"

Delaney stopped and looked at everyone in the meeting hall.

"My dream is to create a people pure and free from all these defects. Mind you there is a financial impact of all these unwanted defects. We have a dream to enhance our people. Preserve a good pool of gene and where possible discourage the breeding and dilution of otherwise pure good genes and the inferior genes. This is common sense. This is the way nature intended. Why in nature the weak mostly are outlived by the healthy? So, you are telling me that because of this they have raised the Hostis Humani Generis claim? What fairness is in that? Don't we have our own rights? How can we be enemies of mankind when we are doing the very same thing nature does? Do you think we would be here today with a pool of great genes if we had listened?"

Delaney looked upset and angry. The men and women looked at each other.

Rex stood up and looked at everyone.

"There is nothing wrong with the improvement of the biological quality of our people. You know I strongly support selective breeding. I support the prevention of the elite's gene pool being diluted and reduced by the inferior genes."

Delaney interrupted.

"So, what is it? Why you are not fighting these accusations?"

Rex looked at everyone at the meeting.

"There are plenty of compelling arguments raised. First and foremost, they are suggesting that your policies and plans are no longer in touch with the world. Mind you we are in the twenty-first century. Whereas the policies might have been widely regarded as perfect in the 1930s. A lot has changed then."

"bullshit. Our values will never change. We have a moral duty to preserve and improve our people. Our institutions were here for more than a hundred years."

"I understand that Sir, but they are saying this is just not to preserve our people but a plan against humanity."

"What's against humanity in trying to improve our people. To control population growth. Relieve the welfare dependencies and be able to control the population. These are the very things nature adopts and implement. We have earthquakes, floods, diseases and famine etc. the very same elements to reduce population."

Janice stood up and handed a document to everyone at the meeting including Delaney who instantly threw it on the table without reading it.

"I don't want to read this. Explain to me."

Rex cleared his throat.

"You should be aware that one of the test subjects has escaped and submitted evidence worldwide over a course of eight years."

"What? How did that happen?"

Delaney looked even more furious.

"Let me finish first. I will get back to that. Like I said they have complied a list of damning evidence. They are arguing that you are deliberately making and increasing these unwanted features so that you justify your plans."

"That's preposterous to even think so."

Janice instantly switched on the huge wall screen and played a video. They all watched.

"Damn it! Find that person."

"Your crime according to the report is that you are implanting, secretly without consent illegally what they are now calling the Remotely Operated Evil Implanted Medical Devices [ROEIMD] even worse than WMD and as such you are deliberately causing these disabilities, these infertilities these genetic disorders through torturing these people hence the *Hostis Humanis Generis term.*"

"They can't prove that?"

They all looked at each other.

"They are arguing that the ROEIMDs are like Weapons of Mass Destruction [WMD]. They are worse than the WMD as they emit a high-voltage electric current, and releases radiation known as bad to human life. They can explode as bombs and above all are implanted by your doctors without consent and against all international codes of ethics. Therefore, as such you are no better than the evil slave traders and the pirates before them."

"They can't prove that?"

"In fact, they are suggesting that your claims about these eugenic plans and your claims about your rights to preserve your people are smoke screens to cover up modern day oppression, torture, exterminations and mass killings."

"Genocide!" shouted Penelope.

Roger stood up.

"They are claiming that through these ROEIMDs you are torturing people and deliberately causing disability and unwanted genes as a political tool to create jobs for your nurses and doctors and above all to provide test subjects you can easily experiment on."

"Using these for research and development!" shouted Janice.

"That's preposterous!"

"Their arguments are that the ROEIMDs are like a coin with two sides. One good and one evil."

Rex stopped and looked at Delaney.

"OK, go on."

"As such even though nearly everyone has one of these devices, they are programmed to provide tremendous benefits to our people and all the unwanted side effects among the other groups. The good side is being applied to our people and you are using the bad side to other groups. Deliberately causing these genetic defects so that you justify your selective breeding policies and perpetuate evil."

"These devices don't come cheap. They are expensive. They can't afford them. This is a simple business tactic. The value you get is dependent upon your income. You pay higher for a service and get higher benefits as well. You don't pay anything of course you get nothing?"

"They claim you are forcing these on the others tricking them which is violating all international laws." added Janice.

"They are saying that you are causing these deliberately. Causing these defects to justify segregation and prohibition of the mixing of genes. In other words, forbidding marriages and mixing. Restricting births among our people and other groups."

Delaney kept quiet.

"You see why everyone is turning against you?"

"I don't care. I made an oath to preserve my people at any cost. I am not God. I am trying to eliminate imbeciles. To reduce population. To reduce the welfare budget. To create a superior people. I believe in natural selection. Above all it's our right to preserve our people and to safe guard our interest."

Janice stood up.

"Sir it doesn't stop there. They are arguing that you are deliberately causing the degeneration of a people," she paused and looked at everyone. She pointed at the video.

"They are arguing that the ROEIMDs are the ones causing the degeneration of genes and all kinds of genetic defects. It is the main thing causing all these defects. A man-made tool. Your tool. Part of your eugenics or selective breeding. Part of your plan. A plan you knowingly and deliberately implemented. A plan you believe in. A plan you aimed at other groups. A plan you have devolved to all those at the bottom levels to carry out and implement. A plan aimed to control population of the other group and as such a genocide plan."

"bullshit! I have rights too. I have obligations too. You know?"

"The third argument is that you are deliberately grooming and rearing these people like chickens using the ROEIMDs as a catalyst to cause defects, speed up aging and speed up death ..."

"Who will do that and for what?" shouted Delaney.

"Organs harvesting. Killing through use of torture tools [ROEIMDs] with aim to harvest body parts of the groups therefore a genocide and the *Hostis Humani Generis notion is* fitting for you."

Janice stood up and waited to be given the chance to speak.

"Your last months' campaign to increase organ's donations and availability mainly from other groups and the number of deaths that resulted from these groups are somehow related. The main argument is that because of a once high shortage in organ transplant among these groups you deliberately targeted to kill and harvest body parts from these groups."

"Like I said these arguments are nonsensical."

"That's not just it. They are arguing also that the underlying fact is that you are trying to eliminate these groups to avoid dilution of your people. This has nothing to do with the shortage of organ transplants. It is inhumane to target the groups even not for the sake of killing them in order to provide body parts but just your evil ways."

"They are arguing also that is it not irony that there has been numerous deaths of people from this group since the launching of your campaign to increase organ donation?"

"The campaign aimed at voluntary donations."

"Voluntary donation? You mean murder and extermination through a direct command by you?"

"Whatever! That does not amount to *Hostis Humani Generis* claims."

"Torture used as a genocidal tool is in fact one of the *Jus Cogens* laws where derogating from these is not permitted at all hence the *Hostis Humanis Generis* arguments."

Rex stood up and walked toward Delaney.

"They are arguing that you are pretending to aim to preserve your people but that the underlying fact is that these are Medical Experiments you are carrying out. Through the ROEIMDs you are experimenting and creating medical advancement in medicines, robotics and in the building of weapons. That questions the morality of all this and as such is now viewed as inhumane because you are using torture."

"You people you have no idea what it takes to preserve a people. You have no idea on how to maintain a pool of good genes. To preserve the elite and avoid the degeneration of the genes. You all sound like you have never heard this before. I think without these measures today might have been ravaged by genetic diseases. I think the world would be a mess with people with inferior qualities. I think there would have been inbreeding and mixing and dilution of the good genes and a degeneration of our people."

They all remained silent and listened.

"Just imagine what would be our welfare budget today? I can say with much conviction that we have preserved a pure elite people fulfilling a promise I made and as such a God given right to look after our own. Therefore, this *Hostis Humani Generis* is ill-founded and cannot stand. It's a give and take situation. What people should be looking are the benefits and if they outweigh the defects. I can declare with much pride that we have seen a high rise in development of medicine. Better methods in the recovery of our soldiers if injured. A new breed of weaponry and above all I have fulfilled my promise to preserve our people and our way of life. We cannot preserve our gene pool if we don't know the causes of these defects. We can't stop the degeneration of genes if we don't use these ROEIMDs to sterilize and restrict breeding among people with inferior genes. We cannot achieve that without restricting marriages among people with inferior and superior genetic makeup. I have a right to preserve and restrict the miscegenation. It's not abuse or the *Hostis Humani Generis* claim."

They all remained silent.

"These people are collateral damage. They were going to die anywhere. I see this as an act of mercy, reducing their suffering. In the processes gaining a better understanding in order to improve our people's gene pool."

Janice interrupted without standing up as the norm or waiting to be given the chance.

"Sir, they are arguing that you deliberately causing

these defects through the ROEIMDs intended to limit fertility. This ROEIMD is the one causing these defects. Through continuous shaking and electrical stimulation and in most cases through torture. In that case justified to accuse you as an enemy of humanity."

"Shut Up! Whose side are you on? Think about our people. We have a duty to preserve our way of life."

"Sir, I think what Janice is suggesting is that there is a thin line between your ideas which might fall in eugenics studies and genocide. It's the same principle the difference is just in the degree of application."

"bullshit. I's pathetic to suggest that our preferences are abusive? What happened to our rights to choose how we live? Nothing is wrong with adopting miscegenation policies if they guarantee the preservation of our people."

Gerald got up and looked at Delaney.

"Yes. Speak up your mind."

"Unfortunately, the world has moved on with the times. It's no longer a ground for defense. Most people use these arguments to justify human rights abuses. Oppression, torture and extermination you name it, but the world is changing. We must change too."

"Our policies and ideas are susceptible to abuse just like the eugenics notions because beauty is in the eyes of the beholder. The ideas and what constitute desired features depends on whoever is in power. The fact that anything other than our people is desirable to us to you then these policies tends to automatically be abusive toward the others."

"Oppression can still exist even if you are providing food and clothes as long as you are using these ROEIMDs to control the people because these ROEIMDs automatically deprive anyone of freedom and infringes on all international laws."

Hailey stood up and walked in front of the hall.

"Sir, with all due respect our policies have been found to be nothing that racial hygiene. Even though this is not illegal but nevertheless it's motivated by racial hierarchy. What we are doing is simply discouraging the contamination of higher elite people by the inferior people. The idea being that if uncontrolled this will lead to rapid degeneration of our people. Having said that, the main arguments are that there can never be eugenics or racial hierarchy I mean our policies without infringements of what they call the *Jus Cogens* laws. In order to preserve the people, you must break human rights laws. Force-on these ROEIMDs and torture people. Force sterilization. Exterminate people who you think have undesirable traits. In-slave the people in order to control the way they breed. Above all to preserve our people and our way of life we must restrict the others not to miscegenate Having said that, I see why one might arrive at the *Hostis Humani Generis* claim."

Rex stood up.

"To conclude this discussion Sir, I want to point out to the definition of genocide. It is a violent political act deliberately undertaken to systematically destroy in whole or part. No matter how you want to look at our policies I think they fit perfectly in this definition. Although these policies are to preserve our people, we are systematically destroying the others and creating situations that will result in their doom. Forced sterilization. Miscegenation policies."

Dennis raised his hand without standing up.

"What is the purpose of an experiment?"

"What? Old man were you asleep? What does this have anything to do with *Hostis Humani Generis*?"

"It's a moral question. They are arguing that this preservation of our people is just an excuse for experimenting on these people illegally. They are arguing that you are no different to the evil Pharaoh or the slave trader. Using the midwives, appointing doctors to torture and experiment on these people."

"If it gives me a better military. If it guarantees recovery times and if that helps the discovery of new medicines what is wrong with that? I am doing these people a favor. Shortening their suffering."

"It's all speculative."

"Sir there is a correlation between use of the ROEIMDs to torture people and disability and genetic defects. Most argue that you are deliberately causing these so that you meet your political agenda."

"You know what? I think I have heard enough for a day. You are all dismissed. I must think this over. I need my space and peace."

"But Sir..."

"You are all dismissed."

"One last point." Shouted Dennis.

"Old man you are the last one always.

"Yes, but I think you should think about this too."

He paused.

"What I don't understand is that if we don't want to encourage miscegenation. If our policies are anti-foreigners. If our policies encourage preservation of our people who we think are a superior people, why do we open the doors to these people? Would not it be better if we just closed our doors. That way it's better to be accused as being selfish that to be labeled a *Hostis Humani Generis*?"

"He might be old, but Dennis has a point. It makes no sense unless what they are saying is true. We can't open our doors so that we sterilize them and restrict them."

"Do you know that our population is an aging population? Alone we have a lot of people dependent on the welfare system. We need workers. Childless people who can work to fund our transport system. People who can work to fund our services. We need people to try our drugs. Where do we get these people? Every economy is driven by these people. What I am disputing is the fact that they are saying that I am an enemy of the people. I might be doing something wrong but *Hostis Humani generis* me? I don't think so."

CHAPTER FIVE

Anthony looked outside and saw the car-park filled with all kinds of executive cars and limousines. He grabbed his portfolio and walked fast into the huge building. He walked down a long corridor. His heart started beating very fast as he approached the huge wooden doors. He stopped and listened for a while before pushing the doors.

"I declare that the accused infringed on my rights and freedoms guaranteed by international laws. These are absolute rights guaranteed by the *Jus Cogens* laws. During a medical operation the defendant secretly implanted a lethal high-voltage-emitting remotely controlled implanted medical device that he is using to torture and breach my rights." Antony paused and looked at the crowd.

"First and foremost, I would like to point out that these issues are real and not imaginary as the accused will try to convince you otherwise. The question of hallucinating is out of the question. In the EU IMDs are regulated by the Active Implanted Medical

Devices Directives AIMDD and this points to their existence but note also that the ones described here might not exist in the open as this is used to torture therefore a secret to them or hidden."

"The ROEIMD is probably a never heard of sophisticated device. Lethal enough to emit high electric voltage and radiation. This device is used for the following five methods of torture..."

Bill interrupted.

"Ladies and gentlemen this is a single case and as such even considering no matter how bad it can be it can never justify the *Hostis Humani Generis* accusations. There is no evidence of mass exterminations, no evidence of systematic widespread torture or human rights abuse for that matter."

"Ladies and gentlemen lack of evidence does not mean that this is not happening. I am going to prove that this is part of a wider political plan and goal on part of the accused to preserve his people at the expense of nearly causing extinction of the group of people. If it's a national policy and part of the fiber of the political system. The command is from the top devolved to the grassroots and as such a systematic and widespread act."

"This is absurd."

"Firstly, I am going to prove beyond doubt the use of torture methods through this ROEIMD. The ROEIMD is a technologically advance device, like I said that is operated remotely and that is being used for hooding, that is blinding someone blind. This device is used to pull the iris of the eye so that vision is lost."

"Who will believe that bullshit?"

"The device is used to hack one's system. This is the same as a hostage situation. It connotes situations of oppression and as such there is no speaking of human rights. A hacker even in computer circles is an illegal person, a criminal if you ask me. A hostage taker is the same as a terrorist. There are absolute rights given by the *Jus Cogens* laws to safeguard our freedoms. A hacked person has no whatever rights or capacity whatsoever to make any decisions and above all does not have freedoms. A hacked person is the same as a slave. The accused is breaking all international laws taking us back to the times when we had no freedoms whatsoever. A hacker just like a master in slave-master paradigm has one goal; to benefit illegally at the expense of a hostage. Just like in human rights abuse, hacking and hostage taking is only beneficial to the master. There can never be a talk of human rights when one is hacked and a hostage. Hacking is done to replace otherwise normal functioning of organs with this ROEIMDs violating all human rights. It is therefore fitting that the accused has been accused of being an enemy of mankind."

"Ladies and gentlemen the accuser broke hospital

rules and as such was punished that way."

"Ladies and gentlemen don't be deceived by this devious and cheating government. I am going to prove that this is part of their racial hygiene policies which are part of and central to their government. Whatever happens on the grassroots level are tools to the means of achieving their eugenic policies of preserving their own at the expense of everything and everyone else."

"The doctors have no direct command from the leaders of the government."

"Ladies and gentlemen, I am going to prove that that is a lie. The doctors and everyone concerned is just carrying out the orders of their leaders. Power and command is devolved. There is devolution of power. Like in the bible there is a striking resemblance to this government and Pharaoh with his persistence of keeping his pure people pure. The same Pharaoh who ordered the midwives part of these physicians to kill all first born in order to curb population growth and to stop miscegenation. In other words, to avoid dilution of his people."

"I don't believe in the bible."

"This is common knowledge as this is throughout history. We have in Sparta in ancient Rome every child inspected as part of this so-called eugenic movement. We all know Darwin's theory of selective breeding. We all know the works of his son and his influence in political ideology advocating for political policies to be adopted for the mass sterilization of 'other' people. Forced torture, etc. The system has not been abandoned but secretly driven-underground and as such is still being carried out using these ROEIMDs which are equivalent to weapons of mass destruction [WMDs]. There is a huge link between his thinking and the government's calling for improved biological gene pools and qualities."

"This doctor acted alone."

"We all know that those inventors who are for this line of thinking lobbied the governments of their times and advised them to form and establish groups of scientists and doctors who will identify those they considered unfit and sterilize these or using torture through these ROEIMDs then segregate them."

"That's not true. Who believes this bullshit?"

"The ROEIMD has satellite properties. That means is used to torture the victims more when they are in certain areas than others causing the people to stay in certain areas hence indirect segregation but still segregation echoing concentration camps."

There was complete silence.

"Ladies and gentlemen. The accused created unfavorable conditions with the aim to cause the destruction of our people in the end. The implanting of these ROEIMDs without our knowledge and consent violates all international laws. It violates the code of practice adopted by the World Medical Association for example and other laws forbidding the implanting of any IMDs that can be used for torture. There is the violation of the *Jus Cogens* laws where derogation is not permitted and as such renders all other acts as void. The hacking restricts some functions. Hacking increases risks of death through cancers as the IMD itself emits radiation. Mind you the accused doctor specialized in Hematology. That illustrates the doctor's devious and bad intend. The doctor cannot plead to ignorance as they know that these IMDs cause these cancers. Looking at genocide's identifying criteria. Article 2-part c states that: *deliberately inflicting on the group conditions of life calculated to bring about its physical destruction in whole or in part;*

"Having said that, I further argue that just like the Pharaoh the accused has embarked on a campaign of tagging all foreigners at birth or throughout their life as part of this Racial Hygiene policy. That means tagging all the foreigners and their children. Like Pharaoh using the midwives and the physicians. This is setting conditions that will make it easy for this group of people to be destroyed."

"Ladies and gentlemen most of these people are refugees and we have a duty to protect them."

"Ladies and gentlemen, you will see the accused for what he is; a devious manipulating crook an enemy of humanity. The ROEIMDs has satellite properties and recording functions and as such is used for torture. Creating white-noises which are played-back as noises continuously just like in white-noises-torture method. Let us not forget that the accused has a very skilled and advanced technology capability and as such is manipulating the space-time continuum or delayed mechanism. This stipulates that with the help of satellite positioning we can go back in space-time continuum to a given-place-time position and playback any recording at that specific place and play these events as if they are happening now."

"That's bullshit. Who on earth will believe this bullshit? Ladies and gentlemen Mr. Antony has suffered a breakdown and has no clue to what he is talking about."

"Let him finish."

"These ROEIMDs renders one immobilized and freedom-less. This is equivalent to modern day human rights abuse. When a person is hacked the talk of freedom and rights is non-existent. Human hacking is the manipulation of the body's system, the nerves, the communication network, the organs through the ROEIMDs that is operated remotely by the master in the slave master relationship rendering the hacked person powerless to an extent of making him a slave therefore the question of that person having rights is therefore unfounded."

"Please! The IMD implanted is like a dog-collar to

achieve behavioral changes."

"Ladies and gentlemen this evil man accused us of hallucinating and he put us through gruesome circumstances without any suspicion that a crime was committed. Now because he has been exposed, he is admitting the implanting of this IMD, claiming the need for behavioral changes, but I want to highlight that this is part of this government's plan and a campaign to purify and preserve their people at whatever cost. All these are means to an end. They are staged. He is a stage-coach. Like a film director secretly threatening the victims and through torture frames the victims. Like in a staged drama from the word go. This is not a coincidence, but a clever calculated plan to achieve his goals his plan. That is channeled from the top of this government to the doctors and grassroots level members. Just like with the Pharaohs. This is a tool of ethnic cleansing. A tool devised to trap the other groups. A tool that will guarantee that he will stay in power without any of the foreigners challenging his position and job. Using the ROEIMDs that have a rotating propeller and are used to rotate and shake the body continuously. There is the increased risk of the 'polymer degradation' as the continuous shaking can result in organ damage. This is intentional to damage the brain of every member of the group so that no one contest his leadership. How can they when they are all mentally incapable? I argue that as such the accused is a great threat to humanity a real-imminent-danger to the group and as such an enemy of mankind. Why then open doors and when people are here then restricting miscegenation? Restrict and curtail others' freedoms in the name of racial hygiene. Having said that, you will notice that their aims are to ill-treat the group, staging traps in order to discredit them as leadership contenders."

"You will hear them argue vehemently that this is their rights part of their plan to preserve their people. A fancy name and morally correct name but still a eugenic policy and as such one that can easily be abused. If all criminals would use that to avoid their crimes, then we would not function as a society."

He paused for a while.

"Ladies and gentlemen the accused is a sophisticated devious and manipulating crook stealing people's savings inviting people and when they are here, then secretly torture them, forcing sterilization, segregation and use these ROEIMDs to torture and then try to harvest their body parts."

There was a moment of silence.

"To cut this short, I argue that we have absolute rights to free from torture. In no circumstances will it ever be justified to torture someone. The accused is arrogant note also that this is not the first time he has been accused of torturing people. If it wasn't for my persistence, he could have got away but thanks to technological advancement as well you will see that from the supplied video the defendant tortured as argued."

"I would put a little weight to all this. No one has ever claimed such bullshit before. In the video he is glorifying how happy he is for the accused to make him feel that happy. A diversion from what he is claiming, acts of torture."

"Ladies and gentlemen how do you corner such a skilled and experienced crook? How can you let him show you his secret so that the world will be able to witness this too? Does not a skilled fisherman place a juicy worm at the end of the hook to lure the fish? Likewise, that was my juicy worm to lure him into telling all of you what he is up to at the same time revealing exactly what he is. A devious, calculating, manipulating enemy of the people. Yes, to add more it doesn't mean that it is not happening. The accused is still in the oppression era only that now it's practiced secretly underground concealed so much that you won't know it exist until you witness it first-hand. Quoting the U.S Food and Drug Administration FDA the person carrying an IMD is prone to attacks that can lead to death. The IMD can be left-open making the system easily prone to hacking, leaving the person vulnerable to attacks. This is a sophisticated genocidal tool creating conditions that leaves the group vulnerable thereby bringing the destruction of the group in the end. The accused is no better than the slave traders and is still involved in oppression even though it's concealed. In *Filártiga v. Peña-Irala,* it was noted that; *Indeed, for purposes of civil liability, the torturer has become like the pirate and slave trader before him Hostis Humani generis, an enemy of all mankind."*

"In this case the accused can't claim ignorance because we have the *Jus Cogens* laws that make it void any acts carried out that conflicts with these laws. The accused is just like the slave-trader an enemy of mankind. Hacking at will to control message, to torture and cause mental and physical suffering. The aim is to cause damage just as in computer circles. The aims of the hackers is to modify or replace physical body system-functions internally through torture using these ROEIMDs."

"This is just speculation."

"Just like a computer hacker the accused is inserting malware electrodes or through rotation of the propeller to change the body functions and manipulate nerves through electromagnetic nerve stimulation. Controlling sexual functions and sterilization the victims. All these breaking all international laws. This is simple to understand. Take a computer hacker for an example and a hacker being a hacker the idea is to inflict harm, modify, delete or add something to cause malfunction. Looking back at the definition of genocide part b states that it is genocide when someone *causes serious bodily or mental harm to members of the group.* The main aim of the accused through use of this ROEIMD without authorization by the owner. The ROEIMD just like in computer hacking has the aim of causing denial of services and functions. The aim is to cause the body unable to carry out some functions forcing it to engage in other functions. This is achieved by the ROEIMD and an electrode fired-in during the operation that is remotely operated. A common practice in electromagnetic nerve stimulation therefore not imaginary but real."

There was silence.

"The accused has carried out snooping, surveillance and illegal information gathering to steal information in the name of preserving his people but a controlling tool and a way of insuring the destruction of the group, controlling population deciding who lives and who dies. Grooming and rearing people like chickens in order to kill and harvest their body parts in the end."

"Like I said this guy is hallucinating."

"The ROEIMD is used to torture by causing sleep deprivation. The device is a rotating propeller just like a small drone is operated remotely but is powerful enough to shake one's body continuously depriving one of sleep. The ROEIMD uses the idea of a bicycle. Having two wheels that rotates all rotating at the same time. One shaking body part like the butt and the other shaking one's brain mashing the brain-up. A form of genocide nevertheless destruction of the people. This should be looked at it the context of the political plan. Their political policies are to conserve their people, their way of life that means restricting any opposition from this group a form of Racial Hygiene. When they all have brain damage and are classed as lunatics no one will challenge them in politics. That guarantees the existence of their people and way of life. A genocide at it's worse. Extermination of a group or rendering them incapable of making any meaningful challenge."

"This is bullshit. He mentioned that everyone has this ROEIMD, disguised under medical records so it can't be classed as targeting your people only. Can it be?"

"Ladies and gentlemen like a coin with two sides what might be good to you might be bad to me even though the method is the same. I ask you to look at my arguments with greater understanding. Like a bicycle the device can be two wheels of the same bicycle. One of the wheels operating on his people for the argument's sake the back wheel and the front wheel operating on the group with the unwanted genetic traits the group being tortured to discourage them mixing and diluting his people. The front wheel is linked to the head. As it spins, it shakes the brain's matter. The back wheel is linked to his people and shakes their buttock's cellulite. Even though this bicycle is the same, being cycled at the same time the effects I guarantee you that they are different. You can't tell me that shaking and reducing your butt's cellulite is the same as shaking someone's brain to a jelly. The accused is a manipulating and devious devil. The title enemy of the people is fitting and as such shall be punished by the whole world. Collective judgment. I therefore declare war unto the accused."

There was a huge buzz.

"Well explained!" shouted a man in the back.

"We all know that the eugenics movement collapsed easily because their ideas lost touch with modern reality, with the rise of human rights campaigners this notion vanished like the morning mist, yet we have discovered that the accused is still at it even though this is still practiced underground and concealed."

"What's wrong in exercising our rights? We have rights too to preserve our people. To preserve our way of life,"

"I am just saying their policies are contradictory and only has one aim to cause genocide of the other group from the word go. You can't claim to preserve your way of life and open doors to floods of people. You can't practice miscegenation, sterilize the people and segregate the people without breaking *Jus Cogens* laws. Unless you are involved in organs trafficking. The fact that there is a huge shortage of voluntary donors this is open to a suggestion that this could be another way to harvest organs. Forced sterilization, human grooming, torture and harvesting."

"Nothing but speculation."

"I want the world to know the accused for what he really is; a manipulating clever and cheating crook. An enemy of mankind using dirty tricks to control not only people but all institutions."

"All the accused is doing is protecting this man."

"On the contrary earlier on Mr. Bill admitted it was a punishment a corrective way like a dog collar to induce behavioral changes. Now he is saying the ROEIMD is for protection. He said I broke the hospital rules. So that proves that the accused is a crook. His initial intention was to kill. To exterminate the whole group. If he wasn't caught and exposed, he was going to kill like he has done before hiding existence of these IMDs accusing people of hallucinating. That fact alone points to a widespread and systematic practice. If it's punishment, you can't expect him to offer sweets. Clearly that fact shows the accused is a deceiving calculating crook and an enemy of mankind using all tricks to destroy other groups with the aim to keep a pure people and preserve his way of life. I would like to add that everyone is innocent until proven guilty. What this accused doing is to trap innocent people first and then according to his policies of segregation and starvation somehow create situations and stage-coach the victims trapping and tricking them to justify the end. The policies are designed to indirectly create a hostile climate and conditions that leads to the destruction of a group. A genocidal act. See Article 2-part c."

"This is not widespread and not systematic."

"The accuser's defendant want just to waste time. I argue that the accused with his policies to preserve his people created an intention to kill, to cause grievous bodily harm, and further the accused took a substantial step to kill by implanting this lethal ROEIMD. Through this ROEIMD he restricted births of the group even though viewed as a population control here nevertheless a genocidal tool. The accused here created a situation when the children of the group cannot be with their parents. All these points fulfills the genocide criteria. The accused is not just a genocidal maniac but a torturer not better than a slave trader. In fact, he is still a slave owner using the ROEIMD to enslave and restrict movements and life. As such it is fitting to address this monster as a *Hostis Humani Generis* and as such I declare global collective attack until there is not even a smoldering stump is left. This crime has a universal jurisdiction. It is every human being's duty to destroy evil without fear of reprisals."

"To meet all the criteria, the act must be widespread and systematic."

"We have already looked at this but to cap I will argue that the accused has a political agenda to preserve his people and way of life. To practice racial hygiene and eugenics as population controls. This is a political idea and as such a party policy that you expect it to be implemented countrywide and as such, I believe in order to control the people they use the ROEIMDs to implement sterilization, segregate people through torture, etc. So, the implantation of the ROEIMDs should be widespread and the torture systematic as well. This is evidenced by the study that once found out that almost half of crematory places has experienced an IMD's explosion. This highlights the fact that it is done is secrecy and the victim's relatives don't even know about it otherwise they could have indicated that on the form they complete that the person had an IMD implanted so that it can be removed first before cremation. This shows that the relatives don't even know."

"Still bullshit. Coconuts if placed in a coffin can explode."

"Coconuts? What a load of a chickenshit. Since when coconuts exploding? Even if they do what are they doing in the coffins? Do you mean IMDs? To further elaborate this point is the fact that the accused is behaving like Pharaoh secretly planning and plotting to exterminate the other group. Hence the secret weapons of death the ROEIMDs. Mind you the accused does not have a legal death penalty, so it is open to us to arrive at this conclusion that the accused has taken the law into his own hands crossing the line and braking all the *Jus Cogens* laws thereby making him an enemy of mankind subject to global attacks from all corners of the earth."

The chairman of the hearing looked at everyone before speaking.

"Ladies and gentlemen, we are gathered here today to hear both arguments for and against the *Hostis Humani Generis* claims and the action to take. I have listened to all the arguments so as the other panel members. I would like to clarify some issues first. I think Mr. Antony has argued that even though this act was against an individual, he has shown beyond doubt that the act was part of a widespread and systematic act. Thus, an act directed at the group. And as such may suffice as it forms part of this widespread and systematic attack. Existence of a plan a eugenic plan, a miscegenation plan, a population control plan whatever or a policy to conserve the people and a way of life helps explain a widespread and systematic act. I am satisfied that he proved that even though the hacking and torture was not carried out by the leaders of the government, nevertheless they had devolved their power to local councils just like the Pharaoh's command instructing the midwives to kill all first-born babies. It is true also that their policies are not different to the eugenics thinking. And sadly, it is a fact that the eugenics had been linked to acts of genocides. The eugenics ideas are easily abused. We have established experimenting doctors using these ideas to justify torture and human rights abuses. There is a clear link between political ideology and the eugenics movement. It is a fact that no matter how fancy and modern the accused want to call his political ideology at the end of the day they are simply eugenics ideologies if not worst forms of genocides. I think we have strong grounds to investigate this in more detail. We will get back to you with our findings and recommendations. I therefore declare the meeting over."

CHAPTER SIX

"How can we preserve our way of life? We have done a lot to preserve our way of life and our people but if the predictions are correct by 2050 our population will have grown tremendously?"

"I think it's not your population you should be worried about."

Delaney looked Charlotte before looking outside the window of the limousine.

"What I don't understand is that why you invite these people when you are concerned about all this?"

"My population is aging. I still need workers to drive the economy and on the other hand I don't want any dilution of our gene-pool."

"But the rate at how this population is growing will definitely be a problem in the future."

"I think the best way is to think ahead."

Charlotte looked at Delaney.

"What are you saying?"

"How do we protect our borders? How do we protect our coastal areas? Imagine all those people coming here. Imagine the impact on services? Do you think you will be able to preserve your way of life? I know now you can because you can contain the people but what if..."

Charlotte looked at Delaney.

"I bet if they flood in, in numbers your way of life and your people all reduced like that [she snapped her fingers] in a minute."

Delaney looked frightened for a minute or two.

"It's a frightening thought. I just don't know how I will do with myself."

There was a moment of silence.

"Do you know that everyone before me was strong and ruthless enough to have preserved our way of life? Surely, I don't want to be remembered as the one who failed. Imagine the curse that will be brought upon my children?"

"Exactly. That's why I am saying that you must be proactive. You must be innovative. Don't leave anything to chance. Hold the bull by the horns. Innovate now."

"What are you talking about?"

"The best human asset is the ability to learn from mistakes."

Charlotte paused and looked at Delaney.

"Isn't that costly?"

"Oh, you know that? So why don't you innovate and start planning now?"

Delaney looked at Charlotte.

"If you are serious about preserving your way of life, you must be innovative as well. The other leaders are not bothered about who visit their country or who they marry whereas these things are central to your decisions. So, you are compelled to act and act fast."

"What are you suggesting?"

"Do you think the global financial meltdown was a coincidence? No. It was part of the Zero-carbon movement plan?"

"Zero-carbon movement plan? What does carbon gases have to do with preserving my way of life?"

Charlotte looked at Delaney and leaned close to him.

"I am not talking about that carbon," she raised her eyebrows.

"Let me put it this way. A few years ago, a huge influx of migrants landed on our shores. Our five coastal areas flooded in no time. You have heard about this?"

"You mean those migrants?"

"Imagine if they have continued flooding like that would our infrastructure and services have supported all of them without any strains? Not. So, we gathered in secrecy to find ways to deal with that."

"Go on I am listening."

"We came up with a zero-carbon plan by 2020?"

"By carbon you mean…"

"Exactly. You don't want to be labeled that word you know. You must be smart as well. Speaking the language Delaney. You can now talk and plan to reduce 'carbon' in front of them. Actually, involving them as well."

"Damn it you mean to say that the Zero-carbon by 2020 is not about carbon?"

"It's about all carbon it's like killing two birds with one stone,"

"Damn it."

"Listen they have grown clever as well breaking our codes and they are very fast as well. So, you must speak and walk the talk. Okay, I was saying that since flooding our coastal areas our five entry points. At first we advised the leaders of countries with these coastal areas to tighten security of these coastal areas?"

"Did they?"

"Human rights and all that nonsense. So, we came up with a plan to send fear and panicking so that they take us seriously."

"What did you do?"

"If they can't work toward a zero-carbon environment, maybe teach them a lesson."

Charlotte looked at Delaney and smiled cheekily.

"You meant you emptied their banks?"

"All five coastal banks succumbed and all these five coastal areas in recession."

"I don't get it."

"Sometimes teaching a stubborn kid actually requires creating that scenario. Shock tactics."

"Where is the money now?"

"We proved they can succumb without us and they did. All five areas with affected coastal areas in recession. The money now ours. Protection money. Now we can protect them."

"Let me get this right. Are you saying that you caused a global meltdown just to restrict migrants flooding our shores?"

Charlotte laughed.

"Of all the people you are the last person I expected to question our motives. We must be innovative in every sense of the word. We can't just sit and wait. This is just not about pressure on our services or infrastructure. This threatens the fabric of our way of life. Especially you, you should be the one advancing these arguments. So far you managed to preserve your people and way of life but for how long?"

"You sound like a wind of change is on the horizon."

"Have you heard about TWO?"

"TWO?"

"Yes. Tomorrow's World Order? I think we are entering a new chapter. The question is are you prepared?"

Delaney looked outside the limousine's window.

"Life will never be the same again. We have swept our sins under the carpet for decades you know that and rolled the ball to them."

"Yeah sure."

"That's about to change. He is digging all shit and throw it in your face."

"What are you saying? But I thought everyone is under us?"

"We have come up with the Innovating to a Complete Zero."

"Wait a minute that's impossible. I thought it's a carbon reduction?"

"Reduction not enough. Total annihilation is the only way forward."

Delaney looked like he had seen a ghost.

"I don't want to be involved. Just a minute ago you said that this TWO is hot."

There was a moment of silence.

"Do you think you can preserve your people forever? Do you think you can preserve your way of life forever? Any increase in numbers will put much pressure on everything. Leaving any stones unturned and now this? Trust me you will not be able to starve them forever. It will be only a matter of time. One day they are going to revolt. A hungry man is an angry man. The more they flood in the more this will become a problem. Innovation to zero is a greater plan. You are taking the course of history into your own hands. You are not leaving anything to chance."

"It's too risky. How on earth can you achieve that? How can you obliterate all and not get caught? There must be something we can do. Increase border security. Build more infrastructure. Provide more services. Invite more females as well. To be honest, I don't care if they marry their own as long as they don't touch mine."

"Delaney you are not making any sense. I think it's worse what you are doing. It's better to just close the doors. Mind you there are a lot of others who can open doors for them and even let them eat their food. What you are doing is inviting problems for yourselves. Nowadays the equal rights movements have become smarter and powerful too. This is a dangerous road you are taking. Imagine if they start rioting. Like I said a hungry man is an angry man. Think about yourself. Your future. Surely tomorrow you are the one who will look for a shoulder to cry on. Wake up. People are fed up unless you are just going to sit in your hole like a wild mouse. If you are to travel abroad, then your policies will get you killed. You don't want to come back in a body bag, do you?"

Delaney sat back comfortably in his seat.

"You have a point. I can't predict what tomorrow holds."

"I am just saying that your policies are contradictory. The human rights movement is sweeping all kinds of rubbish off the ground. This plan is perfect."

Delaney gazed at Charlotte.

"I will explain the basis and arguments behind the plan. A one Kaya, a Japanese energy economist proposed a plan to reduce carbon emissions and save energy. Although this plan is about real carbon emissions, we have used the same plan to reduce 'carbon' emissions."

"I am with you. OK."

"Everyone is worried about how climatic change will affect our way of life. We are worried about how carbon life can affect our way of life. Just like everyone else there is an urgent need to innovate. We must find a new way of reducing this carbon say by 2040."

"Twenty -two years from now?"

"Precisely. Most have proposed reducing the number of 'carbon' but still these methods will never achieve real results."

Delaney looked at Charlotte.

"We argue that unless there is a zero-carbon value climatic change will always be a problem. Unless there is a zero 'carbon' value we will still continue to have pressure on our services and infrastructure and changes in our way of life."

"Charlotte are you suggesting that unless there is no carbon at all there will always be these problems?"

She nodded in agreement.

"Kaya proposed that global warming or problems are the results of a number of people multiplied by services available peer person multiplied by energy per service and multiplied by carbon per energy."

"Some mathematical jargon?"

"Not that hard to understand. To eliminate the problems. Eliminate global warming. Eliminate services and infrastructure issues, problems of miscegenation, degeneration of our elite pool of genes one of the factors I mentioned above must be a zero."

"I understand that. In mathematics multiplying a value by a zero retains a zero."

"So obvious we cannot eliminate our people. We cannot eliminate services or infrastructure instead we should be increasing this. We cannot eliminate services per person. The idea is to increase services.;

Lastly we can eliminate carbon per unit of energy."

Delaney nodded his head.

"If our population continuous to grow and 'carbon' also continuous to grow even if services and energy sources continuous to grow the pressure on services and global warming will also continue to grow. This won't solve the problem in fact there is a limited number of services we can provide at cost efficient way. There is a limited energy sources we can provide but population and 'carbon' population will continue to grow even at alarming rates."

"I get your point."

"But... if we are to get rid of 'carbon' growth altogether we can contain our population. We can provide our services. We can provide enough energy sources, but we can't predict how many 'carbons' will flood our shores."

"{So, eliminating this carbon that way can make us guarantee elimination of global warming altogether."

"Cleverly said. Now I can talk the talk and walk the walk."

They both laughed.

"How do we go about all this?"

"We emptied all the banks," she nodded.

"Lucky you so what are you going to do with all that money?"

"Obliterate 'carbon by 2020' thus eliminate global warming."

Delaney breathed heavily.

"Can you get away with this?"

"It's a perfect plan. We guarantee protection to all our members. All these billions from all banks are now part of the Innovation to Zero Campaign."

"Talking about extermination."

"Do you want to preserve our way of life or not?"

Delaney looked outside the window and sighed heavily.

"Ok I am listening. First, we need a carbon-neutral energy source."

"Meaning?"

"A way of ensuring and aiming to eliminate carbon in source regions. I will explain later. Two we need the capturing of carbon and it's storing."

"You mean the ones we already have?"

"Yes. Don't forget it's innovating to a Complete Carbon-Zero. Thirdly, we must use other methods like nuclear, solar, wind and photo-voltaic even thermal to accomplish our plan."

"It requires more to accomplish that than you have said."

"I haven't finished. We can use the power of terror?"

"You mean as a population control method?"

"Sending terror everywhere. If they see what's in store for them, they are never going to want to have kids anymore. They will stop breeding like animals. That in turn reduces the need to cross borders and come over here. In fact, instead of scaring a few we will eliminate 99% of the population. Reducing the population greatly. Avoiding global warming while working toward a complete zero carbon strategy."

"What do you mean use the power of terror and how are you going to achieve that?"

"Use terror as in terror? Terrorist everywhere?"

She smiled and looked at Delaney.

"The power of vaccinations."

"Vaccinations?"

"Our target is innovating to reduce carbon to zero. Vaccinate everyone now. Each one should be vaccinated even if it means at gun point. To control our borders means do what no one expects or believes is achievable."

"Surely you will get caught."

Charlotte smiled.

"Have you ever heard about the Power of Not Knowing?"

"Not really."

"If you don't know. You will defend and commit to

what you are doing one hundred percent. Only the top people will know. Like a bicycle with two wheels spinning at the same time we shall run this project."

"Meaning what?"

"Meaning we shall run a real Innovation to Zero carbon campaign. Assign it to someone who is trusted by everyone. This person will never know how to talk the talk or walk the walk. It's best if he is in the dark. 'The power of not knowing'. He will passionately implement this plan to give the other plan an alibi."

"OK."

"The other plan. Will be like the other wheel of the bicycle spinning at the same time but differently. This part will make vaccines that will fulfill our plan. All our products will be given to the first plan to actually carry out the immunization."

"Will they won't find out?"

"The power of not knowing. So, this plan let's call it plan A will implement the plan in broad-daylight. He will not question the vaccines or how the vaccines will impact the world. All what's on his mind is work hard make the world a better place for everyone. But we can talk the talk and walk the walk we know. That way for the few skeptical ones he will deal with them effectively for he will defend himself profusely."

"What do these vaccines do?"

"Twenty-two years from now. There will be terror everywhere. The population will be reduced by 99% instead of by one percent as most of the solutions we have today. The vaccines are time bombs themselves."

"Surely you cannot get away with this."

"We getting caught? No. I don't think so."

"Then who?"

They looked at each other. There was a moment of silence.

"Oh, I see but what will that achieve?"

"Re-distributing the resources?"

Charlotte smiled.

"That's stupid. You mean you would obliterate all these people for that? Why not ask people to donate or give something back?"

"Who would listen? Imagine if all the money we are keeping here in the banks was channeled back where it 'came from as raw materials we got cheaper etc.' will we be having these issues? We would not be talking about this zero-carbon. What people don't know is that people are following this money. To solve global warming is to send the resources to areas that have capabilities of carrying the population. Surely these people will follow the money there."

"So, stories about children vaccinated at gunpoint are true?"

"We made them believe that to save them is to save them from themselves but in fact he is involved in mass murder only that he has no clue."

"But why? He worked very hard for what he has in life. I think it's unfair to targeting his fortune just because he has more money..."

"Who is in a better position to help others then? You? I don't think so. That's the only way he will give that away and make the world a better place. What he is doing right now is pretending. Deceiving people and actually causing problems."

"I think that's evil."

"I thought you said you want to preserve your people and your way of life? Are you in?"

"This is using a bio-weapon in broad-light to reduce future population. Extermination at its worst."

"The time people start noticing we will have achieved great. No one is concerned about ten years from now let alone twenty-two years."

"I have a lot to lose."

Charlotte instantly frowned.

"You forgot what happened to us already during the medieval times. The Carbon-death?"

"You mean the Black-death?"

"More than 200 million perished. A lesson for us to pass on. All these countries have developed effective sanitation systems and such a natural population check-mechanism is highly unlikely. That's when we come in. It's our duty. God showed us a way and gave us the brain to see it twenty years from now."

The limousine came to a halt.

"Think about what I said."

Delaney got out without saying anything and looked at Charlotte.

Months later.

A plane arrived at the airport and instantly a lineup of ambulances escorted a huge van at the airport runaway. The van parked near the plane and men wearing overalls covering everywhere that you can't even identify them wearing goggles got out holding young boys and girls before putting them in the van. In the waiting area a woman stood at the window looking outside. A young boy stood by her side.

"Mummy is that daddy? Why is he dressed up like that? Who are those girls and boys?"

"I don't know Taylor."

Other man dressed up in overalls got out of the plane carrying trunks and loaded all these in the van. The man looked on while looking at the waiting room window.

"Come let's go!" shouted the other man.

The woman in the waiting area raised her hand but

instantly touched the window glass. The man looked for a little while before jumping into the van.

The van arrived at a huge compound and the children were taken inside the building passing through water sprinklers spraying them while naked. They shivered while folding their arms close to their bodies. They were then taken into separate rooms where they were clothed. Julia looked lost and scared. She looked around scared and dead worried. Instantly the doors opened and men wearing overalls pushed a sleeping bed trolley into her room. The men just grabbed and placed her on the bed and strapped her onto the bed. They covered her body with sheets before pushing her away. Strapped on the bed she looked everywhere confused and scared. She remembered how life had been. She had witnessed all her family succumb. She remembered being chased by these men in overalls. She felt even more scared. It was not long before one of the men pushed the double doors taking her into what looked like an operating room. She remembered being carried by her legs and hands onto the operating bed from the trolley bed. She tried to struggle, but the men strapped her onto the bed before leaving. Instantly another man entered the operating room and washed his hands. Strapped onto the bed her heart beating very fast she looked around. She tried getting up. Instantly a woman entered the operating room and walked straight to her. The men lifted what looked like a huge silver metal needle. He walked toward her, and they held her down. She struggled before she felt an electrode fired into her left buttocks. She felt the most excruciating pain. When she came around, she was now lying on the other side and she felt a sharp pain on her lumbar bone before she knocked out.

Clara walked into the hospital office. Sydney stood in the office looking outside the window.

"I don't understand why I was assigned to this case. I have just been on my honeymoon. Speaking of instant degeneration or devaluation from a god-to-a -zero-overnight. Do you know getting married increases the status of a person? Honestly, I don't mind taking a pay cut. The risks. I don't understand why me?"

"Stop winging and get on with your job."

"It's easy for you to say what if?"

"They have been processed. You can take over from here."

"I am not happy taking this task. I am expecting as well."

"Clara listen. I assured everyone that it was a good idea to give these children another chance here. All their families wiped out."

"I am just saying that what if we have outbreaks here?"

"Don't be stressing. I said they have been processed.

Anything we can deal with the situation instantly."

"To be honest all this don't make sense."

"What are you implying?"

"I understand they brought trunks full of body parts. If they died like they are saying why even bring the body parts of the diseased here?"

"Maybe you want another honeymoon?"

"I am just saying it doesn't make sense."

"Research and investigations."

"To be honest, I want a transfer to another hospital not involved in all this."

"The situation is contained nothing to worry about. What time are you scheduled to examine them?"

"Two hours from now."

"You know what just to calm your nerves let's go in together. Just to prove to you that it's safe."

"It's okay I will wait. Two hours is a short time. Even three hours I don't mind."

Sydney grabbed Clara's hand and pulled her.

"Come if it means calming your nerves, we might as well do it now."

Clara scared, but a bit relaxed that there was someone to hand in for the slaughter if something goes wrong, she felt relaxed. Julia was fast asleep, but the noise made by the door woke her up She opened her eyes but as soon as a man walked in somehow something happened. Her eye's iris rolled, and she couldn't see even though her eyes were open. Scared to death she didn't even screen she just sat on the bed breathing heavily. Julia followed Sydney scared too until she saw a calm Julia sat on the bed. Sydney suddenly touched the girl's eyes. Clara knelt to speak to Julia.

"Hiya! How are you?"

She touched Julia who was sat on the bed with her eyes closed now.

"Don't be scared. I am here to help you."

She touched her and instantly her eyes opened but the iris was not there. Clara screamed and looked at Sydney.

"Maybe was not a good idea after all. Maybe come back after two hours."

"Is she scared? She is shivering."

Sydney placed his arm behind Clara's back and pushed her toward the door.

"No hold on. I need to talk to her."

Instantly they heard the sound of water hitting the floor.

"It's okay I will bring fresh clothes. Okay."

Clara left and went to fetch the clothes.

"She could just be in shock."

CHAPTER SEVEN

Paige got out of the limousine and walked into the house. She stood in the corridor and shouted.

"Kayden darling are you home?"

She walked into the lounge and removed her shoes.

"Darling are you home?"

"I am in the study!" shouted Kayden.

She pushed the door and saw her husband in the study.

"Why did you come back so early? I was not expecting you until late at night."

"Nothing wrong with coming home early to spend quality time with my beloved husband. I have been thinking about you, about us lately. Just thought I make it up to you."

"Since when you become so romantic? I am not dying you know. It's just a heart transplant."

"No. It's not that darling. I am just horny. I thought I spend time with my husband."

"Oh! That's good then,"

"Okay now that you mentioned it did, they say when you they will get a new heart?"

"Anytime."

"Why did you pay all that money? I thought they had a heart when they asked for all that money."

There was a moment of silence.

"That was to push my position on the waiting list. Donate to this charity and move up the waiting list. Nothing wrong. If you are in my position, you would understand."

Paige looked worried.

"Are we making love or not?"

"I surely thought all that money could have got you a good heart by now."

"All these millions in the bank and still this."

"Maybe go abroad."

"Who to trust? I don't want to end up with a monkey's heart you know. I can trust these people money is nothing I might die and live all this."

"So where are you going?"

"Come let's go to the bedroom where it's comfortable."

Paige felt sad but did her best to hide it. She realized for the first time that even with $millions in the bank life could still be boring. The couple were probably the happiest the days they did wed. Kayden had hit it big. His company was bought for a seven-figure number. That automatically changed everything. After having had that kind of money he felt the need to move to another country. Paige was adamant that that was a bad idea. She had wished to live close to friends who can visit her all the time. Kayden being Kayden he had chosen a total new life with new friends as well. Little had they know that the new country was full of evil people from top to bottom. One routine check-up changed his life forever. He woke up on the operating table with a huge hole in his back but because he was fat, the doctor concerned had pointed to that fact. He didn't feel anything wrong until seven months down the line. One day in his office he heard a familiar voice that really gave him goosebumps. That was a very familiar voice he thought to himself. He got up instantly and walked toward the door and as soon as he opened the door, he opened his eyes but could not see even though his eyes were opened. He felt a sharp knife being pressed against his heart area.

"What do you want?"

The doctor who operated on him started laughing sarcastically.

"No. It's what do you want?"

"Excuse me?"

"Yes. Tell me what you want I am listening."

"You son of a bitch what did you do to me. I want to sue you."

"Not after I have sliced you like a dog."

"You think you can get away from this?"

"You have a lot to lose than me."

"I don't care. I will devote all my life to this cause until I bring you down."

"It will cost you."

"I don't care I have a lot of money."

"OK I am listening. How much."

"How much what?"

"Oh, you didn't tell me what you want?"

"Nothing you swine."

"Don't be shy. Maybe your heart hurts a little."

He poked his chest with a knife slightly.

"Who said that there is something wrong with my heart."

"Oh, I smell a rat. Running away to report me, huh?"

"Let me see?"

"No. Wrong request."

"You son of a bitch. Let me see. You coward."

"I think you need a new heart. I smell too much anger

this heart is not yours. I have a heart fitting for you. Do you know rage can make you die prematurely? Learn to calm down. A soft loving heart will help you a lot. I know you have money, but I just don't know how much you are willing to part away with."

"None. My heart is okay."

The man laughed mockingly.

"For now, but do you know the motor you have is designed after a jet one and trust me the propeller is built to last? In fact, this little thing can take you from a twenty-year-old to a sixty-year-old man in a flash. It can replace your own heart too."

"You son of a bitch I am going to kill you."

The man laughed sarcastically.

"That is if you can see me."

Kayden punched in the air.

"Straining your heart. Surely if that thing starts rotating it's going to stop your own heart."

The man laughed sarcastically.

"Son of a bitch. What is funny?"

"You are going to feel your heart beat everywhere. In your ass. In your stomach anywhere, I want. In that time, we will be weakening your own heart. Changing the rhythm and everything else. Your heart will contract. When that happens, you won't be able even to make love to your wife without increasing the chances of a heart-attack. She will wait for you to fuck her. If I were you, I would buy a dog now. Let her get used to it."

"I am going to kill you."

"When that happens, you will give us your money so that we can give you another heart. That way you will be in our system. All your money will be ours until you are ready?"

"Ready for what?"

The man couldn't stop laughing.

"For harvesting."

"Son of a bitch!"

Kayden threw punches hitting the air.

"You don't know. You brought all your money to us. We never let the money leave our borders. Once it's in, it can never leave our borders. You bought our protection. We will protect you. We will manage your finances. We will tell you who to pay and when. We shall direct you. We shall tell you when you can make love to your wife."

"I will simply take my money and go."

"In this country we don't operate that way. We have accounted for your money in our books already."

"What? How did you know I was coming here? How did you know how much I have?"

"No, I ask you a question. How come you can't see

right now."

"Thieving bastard. I am going to kill you."

"We call it your small-master although most will refer it to as their personnel computer. That small thing will send us all your accounting records. Your account balances. All your transactions. It will record all conversations. All your habits. It can tell us when you want to fuck or not. All this cost money."

"That's breaking all the rules ever written."

"I know but still we don't give a toss. No one has jurisdiction. No money goes out. If you try anything stupid accidents do happen. Let me know when you are ready for a new heart."

"Son of a bitch how many times should I tell you that I don't need a heart?"

"You are not listening to me."

"We provide a whole package. For all that money even more. If you want new pussy here and there, we can get that arranged. All you have to do is ask."

"I am married. You can't talk to me like that."

"You will get used to it. Your wife..." he paused.

"I will kill you if you touch her. Stay away from her."

"My Kayden read the language. You are now in no position to make any threats especially to me. I am like your God now. I control everything. The way you feel. I can make you laugh for no reason. I can make you cry for no reason. I can make you feel the most excruciating pain or make you the happiest man. Above all she is horny, and you are in no position to satisfy her. But don't worry as a down payment we have real men to help her. Consider it as a down payment."

"You touch her, and you are dead. That's inhumane. That's evil. Who on earth would do that to another human being?"

"Tara! Me."

"I will report you internationally. That's oppression and torture surely there are people who will be willing to teach you a lesson or two."

"See we have thought about this. All these institutions are the work of our hands. Honesty no one will even think of funding them. But we can make you disappear, harvest all your body parts and take the proceeds and all the money you have and donate to them. See we have been around for years. So, don't waste your time."

"Surely you can't get away with this."

"See soon you will need a new heart. That thing will never stop rotating. Changing you fast from a handsome man to an ugly man thereby weakening you too. We call it degeneration or reducing you like a price of a bottle of soda from a dollar to a quarter over night."

"I will get it removed I have money you know."

"You are not taking us seriously. We are not stupid. We will simply say that you are waiting for a new heart and you are on the organ waiting list. Where you will end up anywhere. That's protection. That way we are guaranteed that all your money will end up in our coffers and you dead and your young wife with one of us fucking her really hard the way she like it."

Kayden punched the air before leaning against the walls.

"Don't try anything stupid. I know you have a secret son and girlfriend. Surely you don't want them dead. Do you?"

Kayden cried profusely touching his heart.

"Just to get your attention. Man-up Kayden it's not like you are dying. We are just giving you a new heart. But not now. I understand you are scared to get the operation done abroad. In your words; 'in case they give you a money's heart."

Kayden stopped and looked in the direction where the doctor who had operated him was.

"Don't talk to my wife again. Stay away from her."

The man smiled.

"Sorry I haven't had the pleasure of meeting her or talking to her yet."

"So...?"

"You are not listening to me. We know everything you do. We know what you watched last night on television. We know exactly what you did on the internet. We know exactly who you called and talked to over the phone."

"You have no right. You are breaking all the *Jus Cogens* laws that guarantees me freedom and rights from all what you are doing."

"Nobody cares about all that. All the institutions are answerable to us. We fund them generously. All your wealth in tunes of millions and proceeds from the sale of your body parts all for them. Tomorrow we will attract someone else to bring his or her millions and we do the same thing. Unless..."

"Unless what?"

"If he has a son or daughter, then we don't care about him. We know he or she will die soon but it's hard when they are kids. After all the kids will claim rights to that person's money and property."

"That's inhumane."

"I know but hey life is not fair. It's good to us I think no one matters. They come and be harvested and more still come. That's how it is. But organs of young ones last longer than say yours. True?"

A loud scream filled the whole office block.

CHAPTER EIGHT

A van parked outside a big building. The driver went out holding a tablet computer. He punched codes and instantly the door opened. He whistled his way into the building up the elevator until he was on the floor top.

"I have a collection to make."

"I will be with you in no time."

The other man disappeared before coming back with a small box.

"Sign here?"

Soon he was on his way.

The other man checked through the files. Instantly a woman opened the door dress up in white overalls.

"I didn't know we had a delivery. The whole compartment is filled to the top. Just surprised it was empty yesterday."

The man just shrugged off his shoulders.

Months later Kayden jumped on top of his wife.

"I am going to make love to you like on our honeymoon."

"Ya?"

"Off-course. Make it up to you."

"Alright only if you don't make another excuse."

"That thing. They are tampering again."

"You mean your heart."

Paige sat up straight.

"I promise I am not going to make any excuses."

"If you do this time I will go to that place."

"No. Don't. They are blackmailing me so that they offer you another man. I did this for you see." Kayden opened his shirt before removing it. Paige looked at the huge scar across his chest.

"New heart even though I didn't need it. I guess let's just hope for the best."

"You still are talking. You know how much it's hard going through without you when you are here?"

"Come my love. Let us re-live our honeymoon night."

Paige hugged her husband and checked with her hand first. Secretly she smiled. Kayden just knew it. It's now, or she is going to let others eat his food. To him this was worse than a heart attack he had suffered the previous months. He couldn't image another man on top of her. A man who had everything just before that routine check-up. He did his best and for sure he did not disappoint. He secretly smiled the moment she gave an intense orgasm before she fell asleep. Lying down he supported his head with his hand and watched her as she slept. A huge lump of rage moved in his heart. He had to do something about this, he thought. He started caressing her gently stroking her thighs as she slept. Instantly he heard someone scream, but it sounded like the person was very far away. Subconsciously Paige spoke.

"Who is that?"

"Darling you heard that too?"

She nodded. He put on a haunted face but instantly dismissed the idea. All night they made love round after round. After giving an intense orgasm she would fall asleep for a few minutes.

"This is the man I know. Hungry for me all the time and never tired," joked Paige touching Kayden's private parts.

"We are back, and we mean business. I don't mess around me and my soldier we are ready? Are you ready you and your friend?"

Paige giggled holding Kayden's dick.

"Huh!"

Kayden listened to something. He touched his heart. He could not feel his heartbeat. Suddenly, he started feeling heart-rhythms but in his stomach. Instantly his dick lost stiffness.

"Ah. What is going on?" asked Paige.

She looked at Kayden.

"I know how to wake him up. Relax."

Kayden all this time was busy touching his heart then his stomach then his chest searching for his heart beat. Paige was all this time pleasuring her husband but to no available.

"They have started again."

"What? Who?"

Kayden took Paige's hand and placed it on his stomach, then on his heart then back again on his stomach.

"That's strange. Is that your heartbeat?"

One night after making love Kayden slept soon afterward. Paige was still up for it. She lifted his leg slowly and placed it between her legs. She started rubbing on it stroking gently. Instantly Kayden made some slight noises and breathed heavily in his sleep. She stopped and listened for a while. The second he fell back to sleep and had slept flat she continued until a shadow passed by her window. Her heart split into two with fear. She instantly stopped and woke up Kayden.

"Darling I think someone is outside," she whispered.

"Huh? What?"

"I think there is someone outside."

Kayden instantly woke up and looked through the window. Paige got up and looked too.

"Is that a boy outside our house?"

"He is looking over here."

"OK I will go and find out what he wants maybe he is just lost."

"Maybe just ignore. We will check tomorrow morning."

"Don't be scared it's just a small boy what can he possibly do."

Kayden put on the gown and walked out of the bedroom. Paige looked again through the window. The boy was still there. She quickly wore her gown as well and ran after Kayden.

"Where is he?"

Paige looked surprised. The boy was no longer there. They looked everywhere, round the house and in the garden but there was no one.

"OK. Let's go back in the house."

Weeks later Kayden was speaking to his lawyer Georgina in his office.

"I am very sorry to hear that you went through this ordeal."

"It could have been worse. I guess there is nothing important than your life. Money can come and go you know."

"True that."

"What can we do given the circumstances?"

"It's complicated. They have strict time lines. They know that very well. They waited until you can't take them to court."

"Is that why I didn't feel anything the first months?"

"Exactly. They know if you knew within the first months when you have all legal lifeline to sue them then you would successfully sue them. They are deceiving and devious."

"Evil is the correct word. Enemies of mankind if you ask me. Surely there are laws we can play with and get justice."

Georgina stood up and walked toward the window.

"I am afraid not. They know the time limits very well. That's how they are successful. After time limits have passed the only way is the long process and it can take up to eight years for people to start agreeing with you."

"I have the money. Surely these $million can come in handy."

"What would you say?"

"Take this evil to hell if it means with his sons and

daughters so be it."

"So why didn't you?"

"They all joined-in from their leader to the fool at the bottom of the hierarchy."

"International Institute?"

"Useless established by them. All the people in there went through the same way as you. In the end you just give up. Some they have families they just accept it and move on."

"Surely there might be someone who still feels abused like me out there."

Georgina looked sad.

"What will you say? I suffered a heart attack, and they offered me a transplant? Of which they will say you knew the risks."

"No damn it. They abused me. Violated all international laws and implanted this thing without my knowledge. I was in perfect health. I should have listened to my wife. Then they deliberately shook my heart on and off using that thing until my own heart forgot how to pump blood. They replaced a healthy heart with this thing."

"Do you mean with another transplanted heart?"

"No. They implanted something like a pacemaker an IMD I don't know that acted as the new heart substitute?"

"OK I see?"

"Only that this thing renders one a slave. It has a propeller that rotates shaking the whole body or organs non-stop."

He paused and looked at Georgina.

"I didn't need any heart transplant. I was perfectly fine. Then they started blackmailing me. They started controlling everything."

"With this pacemaker like IMD."

"Not just that. I think that same day they fired inside my left buttock's muscle an electrode. Like one used in electromagnetic nerve stimulation. You did science at school. Right? That thing you do with frogs? You know. Passing current so there is muscle plasma or a sudden reflex."

"I know what you mean."

"So, the first days they deliberately paralyzed any organs in my body."

"Are you saying they hacked your system using this pacemaker like IMD?"

"Precisely?"

"What did they ask from you?"

"Threats and blackmail. They said that I will never take the money out of this country. My own money which I brought here or else they will go after it. They offered me their women and requested I give them mine."

"Now that you said that there might be something we can do."

"I am this close in hiring an assassin."

"That won't solve anything. It's institutionalized. The problem I can see is that of the chicken-egg situation, what happened first. It will be difficult to convince people because you accepted the operation in the end. Time has passed. Did you lodge a complaint with any organization who can support your claim?"

Kayden breathed heavily before sitting down.

"I had everything with my lawyer before he died. Guess from what?"

"Shot dead in broad daylight?"

"Heart attack in broad day light. I don't know what to do. All the documents were with my lawyer."

"All I can say for now is that keep trying to trap them. Get some proof. A video or something I don't know. Anything we can use. We need something that shows that first they have hacked you and are abusing you because the intention of all hackers is to cause damage and change. If you are hacked, then you have no freedoms and rights. When all these have been infringed then you are like a slave and it's a master-slave relation. Then we will only need to prove that first its modern-day oppression concealed and practiced underground above all its institutionalized with everyone trying to justify a wrong in the first place. Second, we need to show that this has been happening and is still widespread. If we can prove that it's part of a political agenda, a plan and as such no matter who carried the torture, the whole system is responsible, and we can hold them to account. We must lodge the *Hostis Humanis Generis* as a way out of all this and just hope that someone out there feels strongly about your cause. There are organizations once you prove a *Hostis Humanis Generis* argument they will deal with your case without asking for anything from you. Just doing humanity a favor. This is the only way. Keep on fighting never give up. These crimes have universal jurisdiction. Most people would act on instinctual grounds. We can't live with such evil

in the 21st century. I will lobby all Presidents and Prime Minister of all countries. See how strong your case is. That's the only way to deal with evil. They say evil can only breed evil."

"Thank you. It's comforting to hear that there is a way to get even in the end. I would give away these $millions to an assassin. My life has been turned upside down."

There was a moment of silence.

"So how is Paige?"

"Doing okay. Just another thing."

"Yes, what is it?"

Kayden stood up and walked to the window.

"For the past months we have been waking up at night and most of the time we would see a girl and a boy standing outside our house late at night after midnight. Paige was shaken by all this. We have been everywhere. Now I don't know what to do."

"What did they say to you? The boy and the girl?"

"Nothing. When we go out to meet them, they won't be there."

"Maybe just to spook you out."

She paused.

"Or give me a heart attack?"

Georgina looked at Kayden for a while.

"I don't think so. Just to worry you and frighten you so you donate more money, maybe."

CHAPTER NINE

"Sir someone has lodge a case against you. It does not look good, so they say."

Delaney stood up and paced in the study.

"Who is that fool?"

"A one Kayden."

"Oh Mr. Kayden. He has not learnt anything has he?"

"No. I don't think so, Sir."

"Assign him to me."

"Are you sure Sir? I can deal with him myself."

"Are you sure?

"That will be okay, Sir."

"Get ready then."

Paris sat down in Delaney's office.

Instantly the door opened and a man carrying a laptop entered in and sat down He typed very fast before a message startled all,

'Synchronizing successful. Initiating the program.'

Instantly Paris stood up and walked to the chair where Delaney was seated.

"Hang on. Hang on. Let me get up."

Delaney stood up. Paris sat down and stretched her legs lifted them on the table.

"I love you Paige. Once all this is over, we should take a short break from all this. Maybe spend time together." said Paris.

Delaney and Peter just looked on.

"How long you want this to go on for?"

"Let the program run for a while then switch to the robot." replied Peter.

"OK. I will spend the day with her send the robot to my house,"

"Okay, Sir."

Delaney sat in his office listening to all what Paris said and did that day.

Kayden got out of his limousine talking on the phone. He entered one of the shops in the city. He looked around admiring the jewelry. A sale assistant suddenly approached him.

"Can I help you Sir?"

"Sure. I want this for my wife."

Kayden left the shop and walked for a while talking on the phone. Instantly he stopped and instantly dropped his cellphone down gob smacked. In front of him was a little boy. Surely, he had seen this boy before probably the reason he looked shocked and haunted.

"You! What do you want? Can you speak?"

The boy remained standing there. Kayden knelt and looked at the boy. The boy stretched his hand to touch him but instantly Kayden felt someone touching his shoulder and lifting him up.

"Sir are you okay?" asked Lauren.

Kayden looked at Lauren and then at the boy.

"Come on Sir. Let's go."

"No. I am okay really. I was talking to this boy."

"Do you know him?"

Kayden just looked at the boy.

"Mama." whispered the boy looking at Kayden.

Kayden looked at Lauren and the two looked shocked.

"What did you say?" asked Lauren kneeling in front of the boy but the boy looked behind her looking at Kayden and stretched his hand.

"Mama!"

Lauren stood up and looked at Kayden.

"It's time to go Sir."

"Let's take this boy with us."

"No Sir. Let's go."

Kayden and Lauren walked to the Limousine.

Kayden looked shocked and sacred.

"Don't worry Sir. I think his English is not good." Kayden relaxed for a while.

"That makes sense. That kid nearly gave me a heart attack."

Lauren looked at Kayden's heart area. Kayden pulled out his wallet and took out money.

"Give him this."

Lauren took the money and got out of the limousine and walked toward the boy.

"Take this."

"Mama," said the boy looking at the limousine.

Lauren looked at the limousine and then at the boy.

"What is your name? Can you speak English?"

The boy remained silent.

Lauren started walking back to the limousine.

"They killed my mama," said the boy.

Lauren looked at Kayden who was staring at her when she overheard the boy. She didn't turn around to look at the boy. She continued walking toward the limousine.

"What did he say? I thought I heard him say

something," said Kayden.

"Nothing he can't speak English."

The limousine left headed out of the city center. Kayden and Lauren just stared at each other without saying anything.

The limousine arrive at Kayden's residence. He got out and waved goodbye. He looked at the bedroom window and saw his wife looking at him. She looked at him but did not smile or even wave at him something she normally did instead she looked over the road. Kayden looked at her for a while before looking in the direction she was looking at. She saw a boy standing there looking at the house. She looked closer. It was the same boy or another but wearing the same clothes. Kayden looked at his wife and she pointed at the boy. He got the idea. He started walking toward the boy while his wife watched from the bedroom window. His heart started beating very fast with every step. He looked at his wife and saw that her eyes were fixed at the boy. When he was closer his cellphone rung startling him. He stopped and looked at the identity of the caller. It was an anonymous identity. He answered the phone.

"He can't speak English. He doesn't want your money."

"Who are you? What do you want from me?"

"Me. Nothing. But the boy maybe..."

The caller laughed sarcastically over the phone.

"Don't play games with me. Don't call me ever again."

"Madam! Madam," taunted the caller over the phone.

Kayden stopped and looked at the bedroom window. His wife was pointing in the direction of the boy. He turned around and started walking back to the house.

The phone rang again.

"You got his mother killed...."

"What? I was on the waiting list like everyone else."

"You flashed your money at us..."

"Don't call this number again."

Kayden looked at the bedroom window. Paige was hysterically pointing at the boy. Kayden looked in that direction and saw the boy walking away. He stood there until the boy disappeared. Paige ran downstairs. She opened the door.

"Darling you should have talked to him. Why you let him go. You don't want to know what he wants?" Paige ran after him.

"Darling! Darling! Let him go."

Paige stopped and stood there for a while.

"They have always disappeared. This was our only chance to get answers and put this behind us."

"I know. No point. He can't speak English."

Paige hugged her husband, and the two stood there

for a while.

"Come let us go inside the house."

"What is this all about? The operation."

"I don't know darling."

Paige entered the house and headed straight to the bedroom leaving Kayden in the lounge area. She threw herself on the bed. Kayden remembered the look on Lauren's face. Surely there was more to what she said. Surely, she was hiding something from him.

He walked up the stairs to the bedroom. He pushed the door and stood at the door.

"Maybe you were right."

He walked in and sat on the bed.

"We should never have come here. I should have listened to you and stayed close to my friends."

"What difference does it make maybe we should go back?"

"We might lose our money. They threatened to kill everyone."

"Just transfer the money out. Buy another house out of this country they can't stop us."

"Sit up straight I have to tell you something."

Kayden touched his wife.

"Today I met the boy in the city center."

"The same boy who was outside?"

"I think it's not just one boy. They are trying to blackmail us."

"What did he say?"

"He can't speak English. But..."

Paige looked at her husband.

"He only said mama."

Paige looked at her husband.

"Oh. I was with Lauren."

"Oh. I see."

"We have to sell this house."

"I will send our money abroad."

The couple made love and Paige fell asleep. Kayden breathed heavily and opened his laptop. He started researching about the hospital that carried out the operation. It seemed everything was legit. He put the laptop on top of the dressing table and slept too.

"Darling I have to go see you at night. I love you."

Paige woke up.

"You are going already? Maybe take time off today?"

"I can't today. I have to organize the transfer and all that stuff we talked about last night."

"I love you too."

Paige slept again.

A beep sound woke her up. She looked at her phone.

She looked at the dressing table and saw Kayden's laptop. He had never left this laptop before. She noticed that a message or something had activated the laptop from the sleep mode. Maybe Kayden's business message. She slumped back to sleep.

Another beep sound startled her. She raised her head and looked at the laptop screen that was half-shut. She slept again. Instantly a clip started playing.

"Mama! Mama!" shouted a boy's voice.

Instantly she woke up and grabbed the laptop. She looked at the video. Instantly her heart split into two.

She took the laptop and left the house into her car and drove off. The car over took other cars speeding away. She turned into the airport car park and got out of the car. She ran up the stairs to the lobby. She stood at the window looking outside to the runaway. She walked to the receptionist.

"I need some information of a flight that arrived here on Friday 23 November last year."

"Last year? Even if it was yesterday, we would not be able to tell you. Maybe try ringing the airline itself."

"I don't know which airline it was. But I know the time and date."

"Best contact customer service. Use the direct phone over there."

After a while talking over the phone Paige walked out of the airport. She took out her phone and dialed a number. Later that afternoon She entered the hotel lobby and bought a soft drink and walked to one of the tables. She looked around before sitting down. A woman in an expensive suit arrived into the hotel lobby and walked toward Paige.

"Mrs. Paige."

"Do I know you?"

"You phoned."

"Okay..."

"Yes. Stop all this you will only get hurt either way."

"Sorry who are you again?"

"Let's just say your worst enemy."

"Either way I am going to find the truth."

"The truth will only destroy you. You think we are stupid?"

"No but you think I am stupid."

"Stupid. I would not use that word. I would say you are still in the dark and honestly you don't know what you are dealing with."

"Whatever it is it will destroy you too."

The woman leaned very close to Paige.

"Human trafficking. Dealing in illegal organ harvesting. Torture and extermination charges not mentioning testing of bio-weapons on unsuspecting third world countries with the aim to harvest organs.

Surely you will pay more than us. After all you are going to steal our money, anyway."

"Listen to me very carefully. You don't know what you are messing up with."

"I will say the same to you. There are international institutions willing to do something about this."

The woman laughed.

"You think I am bluffing?"

The woman touched Paige's shoulder.

"You know what? We are already prepared for you and your husband."

"I know and to be honest you are going to kill us in cold-blood, anyway. So, I don't care."

"It's more than you thought."

The woman took out photos from her handbag and threw these on the table. Paige looked at her first before taking and looking at the photos. Instantly her heartbeat elevated.

"What's this?"

"Exactly. The same question everyone will want to ask too and get some answers."

Paige thought for a while looking at the photos.

"I will still prove that somehow you are killing these people. Extermination at such a scale to harvest organs is a big deal and most news agencies will pay huge sums to get such a story. Easy way to recover our money."

"And say what? That you received Ebola victim's organs?"

"We will ask what organs of Ebola victims are doing here in the first place? I will prove that you are creating symptoms in all victims like those caused by the real Ebola disease, but you are using electricity to induce these symptoms. Everyone knows about nerve manipulation through electromagnetic stimulation using an electrode implant. I will prove that your main underlying goal is to kill and harvest organs."

"It will take a lot of convincing by the time they realize that you and your husband will be dead."

"We will take our chances you are going to kill us, anyway."

"You are looking at genocidal charges. If people know exactly what you are doing, I think the world will revolt."

"We will simply say that this was a bio-weapon that accidentally escaped. Mistakes happen. By then your $millions will be ours and we can give that away as compensation mind you all these people are too poor to do anything."

"What are the international courts for?"

The woman smiled and touched Paige's lap.

"My dear. Like I said you are still in the dark. What

institutions?"

"The Global Court and the International Global Court."

"What the world does not know is that we created these courts. These courts are funded by us. These courts are run by our people to give us immunity and an alibi by prosecuting the low-level-often poor perpetrators. Do you think we would get away with this if there was a real power to deal with this? We make deals with all these low-level perpetrators. We fund them to cover-up for us on condition that no one touches them when still in power they will only pay when they are old and ousted. That way we all do what we want and continue with our way of life. Ask your husband he will tell you the importance of our organization."

"You blackmailed him."

"Nothing for free. He was clever enough to acquire such wealth, but we made him realize that all that is useless. He was prepared to give us all his millions just for a heart."

"He is not stupid. He has already lodged a case," the woman smiled.

"We know. That is why you are now seeing those children."

"You sent them?"

"Do you think this is a coincidence? It is a planned

and tested method to bring your destruction."

"I don't think so. We sent proof everywhere that the organs were clean. We can also prove that you are using nerve stimulation through electromagnetic stimulation to recreate these symptoms otherwise there is no risk from the organs but just a clever plan to hide extermination at an unprecedented level, genocide in short, oppression, trafficking and prostitution selling these babies to the highest bidders and grooming them."

"Who will believe that?"

"We can prove that it's obvious. Your ideology of preserving your own at the expense of others is the main drive. The same ideology to restrict 'degeneration of yours' by foreigners, made you kill in order to harvest body parts with the aim of using these organs for blackmailing and killing the rich foreigners and stealing their wealth once they have settled in your country."

"You are clever."

She smiled.

"We are going to kill your husband. Torture him to death and then blame it on the transplant and admit there was a mix up."

"Not after I have exposed you."

"If I were you, I would not."

"Why?"

"We have 'reduced you' in value as well. That way our policies of eugenics can be accepted as needed and vital to protect our people from contamination by foreigners like you."

"You mean you are making bio-weapons to kill and use body parts to make money and blackmail people? You abuse needlessly and justify outdated ways of thinking. This is the twenty-first century why not move with the times? You are like snakes you just bite things you don't eat."

"You people never get it. Preserving our way of life means keeping the way things were a thousand years ago. If it means using dirty tricks so be it."

"We know you are very clever, but we have a plan in store for you."

Paige smiled.

"We are above everyone. Untouchables. Global Court and International Global Court will all tell you that they have no jurisdiction."

Paige smiled.

"I know."

"So, if you know why you are then wasting your time?"

"Let's just say the world is going to change for the better after this?"

"Planning to go somewhere? I understand that your

husband is busy transferring money abroad as we speak?"

"You can say that."

"You didn't get me. I said that your husband has a heart of an Ebola victim. That puts you at risk as well."

The woman sat comfortably in her seat expecting Paige to be afraid.

"Look over there. They are taking pictures of you and me as we speak. I recall your people spent a lot of time with my husband as well especially the doctor. If he is still alive then what risk will there be? That means for claims to succeed in court you must die first forcing them to kill you too. That's being clever too."

Paige waived at a man far away taking pictures as well before the man disappeared. The woman instantly stood up and started walking away.

CHAPTER TEN

David walked to the window and unfastened his tie. He fumed with rage.

"What do you suggest then Sir?"

"I said this court thing is useless. A waste of precious time. What do you think the Global Court and the International Global Court will do? They will simply tell you that they have no jurisdiction."

"What are you saying? Are you saying that they are incapable of solving global injustice?"

"Damn right. They are created by the very same people responsible for the worst crimes. They put on trial only the weak and the poor. To make things worse, they put on trial only the ousted. What is that good to us? These courts are outdated and passive. We want an organization that has power. We want Tomorrow's World Order {TWO} to making these people sit down. We want a proactive structure that has powers to eliminate immunity of those who commit rights abuses. We can't wait until these people are frail to put them on trial, we don't want to wait for these culprits to travel abroad and expect the other country to arrest them. TWO has powers to go and dig out the culprit whether they are in power or not. Ladies and gentlemen if you are serious about solving global problems. If you are serious about eliminating injustices. If you are ready for a one world. If you are ready for equal rights and a just world. A better future for everyone. A better place for all humanity then you will agree with me today that TWO is ready. That TWO is the only structure that will solve these problems. The only structure that will not only put a stop to this but the only structure that will guarantee that this will never happen in the future again. All global issues are there because these culprits are creating problems to better themselves at the expense of everyone. They are making bio-weapons to kill. First to harvest organs. Secretly to reduce their long organ waiting lists. They are playing God killing to reduce population but who are they? They are using bio-weapons to displace the population and gain all the skilled migrants leaving the abandon areas without any skilled workforce. They are using bio-weapons to cream resources from all over the world. People are selling their houses and using the money and all life-savings to fund their airlines. To bring all the wealth to their countries. Above all this then disadvantage these people through their eugenics policies. Furthermore, they are using bio-weapons to segregate and discourage miscegenation. They are using bio-weapons to blackmail foreigners to give up their riches before killing them. These people are the ones making weapons of mass destruction killing thousand in the tune of 500 000 in broad day light and walk away with it. But ladies and gentlemen TWO...."

He paused and looked at everyone. His silk shirt clanged to his pumped-up body. The more he talked, the more he got even more ripped. It seemed his muscles were growing with every word he uttered. Everyone listened attentively.

"Yes, TWO is going to set the record straight. Yes, TWO is the only answer. TWO, ladies and gentlemen will put a stop to all this. TWO will see to it that the world shall be a better place for everyone. TWO will make everyone accountable. Yes, TWO will bring perpetrators to justice. Yes, TWO will ban making of bio-weapons unless we get invaded by aliens. Only then will it make sense to make and use bio-weapons. If it's only us humans. TWO will ban bio-weapon's production across the whole globe. No one shall have immunity against *Jus Cogens* laws. These laws are universal. These laws shall not be broken. TWO shall make everyone accountable."

The people started clapping hands.

"The solution to all today's problems is one simple one."

He unfastened his tie even further and wiped the sweat drops using his towel.

"Today's problems are all rooted in one idea. Yes, believe you me when I say all our problems are caused by a mere fact. Yes, all world problems are simply because we still see differences. Yes! Simply because we see differences."

He paused and looked at everyone.

"We have a war today simply because we see differences. Some people are aliens to us. We are still not united even though we are all humans. We chose inferior thinking despite 2000 years of existence. We make bio-weapons today because we see differences. Other are still aliens to us therefore we feel that we are more at risk of being attacked. We build footrests because others are still aliens to us. We protect ours because we see differences. Whatever our sole reason if you look deep you will notice that it's simply because we see differences."

He paused and looked at everyone.

"Think of any ten global issues that come to mind and I will tell you that 90% are caused by the simple fact that we as human we see differences. Okay any ten. Yes Sir."

He pointed among the people.

"Global warming, Poverty, Conflicts, Inequality, Corruption, Unemployment, Illiteracy rates, Security, Lack of food and water and global financial stability."

"All these are direct or indirectly a result of us as

humans instead of being the superior beings and eliminate all differences we still see and perpetuate differences."

Someone raised his hand.

"Seeing these differences is what actually drives humanity. Probably the same reason God created so many variations. So, in fact seeing these differences might be a single factor determining our existence. Capitalist thinking is to make whatever you have different from the other person's in order to survive the competition. Ignoring these differences lead us back to socialist thinking."

There was a huge buzz.

"In some way that seems true. If you admit also that you are an average thinker, and this is the best you can do. If you think inferior, you will always get inferior outcomes. But it takes a bigger brain to be superior and act in that and see past these differences. Animals see these differences for their survival because they can't communicate with other animals. Above all these animals depend on other animals to survival. In other words, they are part of their food chain. Whereas this is totally different with us humans unless you guys have developed a taste for each other."

The people laughed for a while.

"It's understanding the context. Animals must be serious capitalist because they fall in each other's food-chains. Humans could have been serious capitalist if we had aliens. But surely if it's human to human there is no need to see differences. For a thousand years we have carried on ideas generated when we had aliens."

The people laughed, and a huge buzz filled the conference hall.

"Yes, what do you call the dinosaurs? Surely humans had to be excessive capitalist to survive. But all these guys, the dinosaurs etc. have long been gone. Surely that calls for a change in a way of the way we look at things. We still rely on methods used 2000 years ago. Surely what worked then cannot be expected to exist and be relevant today. Our thinking is defensive thinking. We see differences and everyone else is alien to us. But ladies and gentlemen the other guys [dinosaurs etc.] have since given up so why are you still stuck to this inferior thinking. Take any budget of any country. Look at the proportion that is spent on military. Defensive thinking. But who is our enemy? Dinosaurs? Our neighboring countries?"

"We have the right to protect ourselves in case we get attacked. What we spend our money on is none of anyone's business."

"But I will assure you also that there is corruption and inequalities in your country. In fact, you use the defense reason to cover up your incompetence and you still see differences. You would rather build a weapon than solve pressing problems. Still inferior human thinking."

He paused.

"Every house has a head of a house. A school has a head teacher. A university has a chancellor. A city has a mayor. A country has a President or Prime Minister. But the globe has no leader. Everything function well because there is someone to solve all the problems. We have other countries that have assumed the role of this global leader."

A huge buzz filled the hall.

"Yes. I am Hudson. My country is the global leader. I have assumed this position and what you are doing right now is duplicating roles. A waste of time and money. Where there were abuses, I have personally assumed responsibilities and did send my boys to destroy these motherfuckers. We have a track record to prove that. Ask anyone here who they turn to for help? Me!"

Hudson pointed at himself and looked at everyone nodding his head showing off.

"This is no joke. We anticipated this, and we were quick to act. We have the highest spending of any country not because we are stupid. No. We are the muscles these countries turn to when their leaders abuse them. We are proud and hope to continue to do the job. It's a pity you don't appreciate our efforts you would replace the mighty wings with this TWO.

Where do you get the resources for a war? A war cost a lot you know?"

David listened attentively and walked to the center of the hall.

"Thank you, Sir, for all your efforts to purge evil. I agree with you, but it is fittingly correct that TWO takes over."

"Wait, a minute. You are just duplicating roles. This is absurd."

"The world need a global leader. A leader recognized by all. A leader trusted by all. A leader still with everyone's trust and respect."

"All that you said young- man. Me? Just describing me."

Hudson stood there boastful and looked at everyone.

"Reputation and trust is of paramount importance in politics. We are talking about a global leader. A leader to solve global issues and problems. Sir."

"Yes, all me. Son."

"I am afraid that I can't say the same anymore. You have been tainted with blood of women and children in the tune of 500 000."

"What are you talking about son?"

"A man owed his friend some monies. The man asked for his money and the man had no money but had an idea that will get him that money. So, he asked his friend to go with him, so that he can get his money back. Although he disagreed with the idea, he still went because he wanted his money back. Women and children got killed. He later realized that his friend had set him up. He had killed women and children in cold-blood for nothing. His friend although he swore that he had no idea that women and children were going to die deep down all this was a calculated plan to get his friend hooked and be able to be his wing-man no matter what."

"Nonsense. That's bullshit. He is my friend and can never do that to me."

"I am afraid Sir. Your friend is calculating and devious. What he did is make you his forever.

"Nonsense! I am the most important man in the world."

"Was the important man in the whole world. I agree. But 'was' in the past."

"What changed? I am still the same man. The man everyone look up to as their leader.

David shock his head in disagreement.

"You are now like food in a store labeled 'NOW REDUCED,' a common practice with your friend."

"Me 'Now reduced' bullshit."

"Yes, a minute, a split second ago sure you were the most valued and admired leader but within a second too you simply became the 'Now Reduced'. In other words, you were instantly weakened."

Hudson found it hard to contain his anger. He lifted a glass of wine and squeezed it hard until it disintegrate into pieces. He shook with rage.

"Sorry Sir but your friend tricked you. He lied about the intelligence to get your approval but even more sadistic to reduce you so that he has a more bargaining hand in negotiations."

"Bullshit! Do you know trust and loyalty in our circles? He would never drag me into something like this. Killing women and children for nothing."

"There is more to that Sir."

Hudson took out a handkerchief from his pocket and held his hand.

"The main idea is that for years people had accused him of human rights abuses."

"What does that have anything to do with me?"

"Let me finish. For years people have complained about abuses at the hands of your friend. People have been tortured. People have been enslaved by this friend of yours. He knew time was running out for him. You-being-you he knew that only you as the global leader will be a real threat to him. He knew your outstanding record on human rights and defending the weak and the voiceless."

"What are you saying?"

"You being a man you are. The leader of the people. A man of character. A man who listens. He knew that one day things were to catch up with him."

"But this guy is my friend?"

"Exactly. He also knew you very well that if you are to choose between what is right and him you will go for what is right at his expense."

There was a huge buzz in the hall.

"Son of a bitch!" shouted Hudson.

"So, to guarantee his safety and his continued existence and to continue torturing people and abusing human rights he had to taint your hands too."

"Kill innocent women and children?"

"Precisely. This is the monster your friend is. Today I stand here in front of all these people and say this friend of yours is more-evil than you think. He will cover up his ass at the expense of these children and women. In other words, his crimes are worse than killing 500 000 women and children. He knew if you are involved and your hands also covered with blood, you will not do anything and will never attack him, so you and he are now the world's worst enemies."

"But people know I am clean. I will never deliberately kill women and children or misrepresent facts."

"True Sir. We know that we believe that but still women and kids died Sir."

"You took the money you had borrowed him. But this money was guaranteed by contracts signed after the killing of women and children."

"He owed me money. He misrepresented intelligence."

"We know Sir that explains Tomorrow's World Order. Your hands have been tainted with blood. Still you are still together with this friend of yours. Where ever he goes you will go too Sir. People today now speak of evil cults. Cults that will do anything and cover up everything to protect themselves and protect their friends. Sir with all due respect would you say that same person is fit to be a global leader?"

David looked at Hudson.

"Sir, would you say that person can still be called a global leader?"

"It depends. I liberated millions from evil. I carried out many operations that are morally correct you mean to say that this one event would change that?"

"I am afraid so yes Sir. Because you are still together what if tomorrow, he tricked you again to kill innocent people to cover your back?"

Hudson looked down. Everyone else looked at him.

"What I can say is that you don't know your friend very well. In fact, he is not worthy to be called a friend by you. Your friend is an enemy of mankind. A person who will deceive a friend in order to kill innocent women and children just to 'reduce your power as in weakening' is a bad friend. This friend is a manipulator. His ideas are rooted in viral-mutations ideas, in weakening and reducing everyone around them so that they can do what they what. In that case he wants to control you. After weakening you. You will be under his control. Having said that, we all know he is evil. We also know that your acts to uphold the rule of the law were outstanding but nevertheless having said that it is with much regret that you no longer have power and control regarding him. Every decision you make will be his decision. You are under his spell in such circumstances that now we believe you will do whatever he asked you to do. In that regard I declare you unfit to be a global leader."

"But..."

Hudson looked at everyone in the hall.

"Bastard! I am going to kill that bastard!"

"What did you just say Sir?"

"I will kill that son of a bitch!"

"That's the spirit but you must understand Tomorrow World Order is a new and fresh start to tackling global problems. Unless you untainted your hands we have slim chances of working together."

"Now I understand why my predecessor wanted to kill this bastard. I swear I will do anything do cleanse my hands."

"Distancing yourself from him is the first step Sir. But you will have to do a lot more to achieve approval rates again."

"As long as I live, I will do what is right even if it means fighting this evil."

"We need more from you. You will need to convince the world that you are willing to destroy this evil. To stand for human rights. To donate back to the families of the victims and above all distance yourself from all these cults. I bet all have been tricked just like you."

"I swear I will not be involved with these evil cults again. From today I shall attack all evil even if it means leaving these cults so be it."

The people stood up and started clapping hands.

"Ladies and gentlemen give a big applause to Mr. President Hudson."

Hudson sat down and started applauding as well as David walked to the middle of the hall.

"If it wasn't for the lack of confidence and trust in the current global justice system, I bet President Hudson would have been an outstanding global leader. But let's face reality. Today evil cults are going unpunished despite the century's gross moral decadence. Today no one value the lives of women and children. Today I stand here and declare war to any man who will declare wars that kill more women and children than solve anything else. Today I shall make it a law that will value the life of any woman and child out there. No one shall kill even for the purpose of toppling a dictator. Why kill thousand as well in order to kill one. We shall implement a new method that will judge each mankind separately. Today I announce our new weapon against evil people. Today I the President of Tomorrow World Order I introduce a new weapon to maintain law and order. A new weapon that will make the world a better place for everyone. A new weapon that will see no need for making weapons and spending billions on weapons. TWO will bring peace and total respect for human life especially the life of innocent women and children. Today I give you the Inbuilt-Gun. This will be made compulsory,"

There was a huge buzz.

"Mr. President."

David smiled briefly.

"The first person to address me as your President. I am pleased and honored to be a global President to address global issues. We all agree that today's global justice system has been corrupted and abused. After all these institutions were created by the same people, we are saying that they have abused the *Jus Cogens* laws. These institutions are just there to perpetuate injustice. To perpetuate the existences of these people and their way of life. To continue to abuse women and children. To continue to torture, breaking all the international laws. Today ladies and gentlemen I am honored to be your global leader."

Mr. Dominick the Prime minister of another country got up.

"Where would you get the funding for weapons? You have no territory you control I control my country where will be your offices? Mars?"

Everyone laughed.

"A very good question."

He paused and looked at everyone.

"Ladies and gentlemen, do you want global problems gone??"

"Yes!" shouted the leaders.

"Ladies and gentlemen, do you want a just world? A better place for every child. Yours or mine? A better justice system?"

"Yes!"

"I believe you want evil cults gone!"

"Yes!"

"Ladies and gentlemen, you want real women and child killers gone!"

"Yes!"

"Do you want a torture free world?"

"Yes!"

"Do you to see a disease-ridden-world gone!"

"Yes!"

"All bio-weapons production stopped?"

"Yes!"

"All dirty tricks gone!"

"Yes!"

"Ladies and gentlemen above all do you want to see the enemy of mankind obliterated?"

"Yes!" shouted the people.

"I repeat do you want to see the *Hostis Humanis Generis* Extinct,"

"Yes!"

"Then all the weapons you have will belong to Tomorrow's World Order. Who shall destroy them?"

"Destroy them?" shouted the people. There was a huge buzz. David stood there for a while letting the people talk.

"The weapons are worth trillions of dollars!" shouted the leaders.

"Isn't that the reason why you made the weapons?"

"We thought.... we will be attacked."

"So maybe we use all these on the enemy of mankind. The real child and women killers. A torturer. A genocidist. Someone who will deceive and misrepresent facts to cover his ass at the expense of women and kids. Someone who will kill so he can steal resources to pay the debt when we sweat our ass off for that. A person who will take us back to the medieval times when disease was the worst threat to mankind. Remember the Black death? Who in their rightful mind would try to re-create that without becoming a *Hostis Humanis Generis?* I say today is another chapter in mankind history. Today is a new start. We cannot move forward. Our real enemy will never change. He will deceive us and misrepresent again just to cover his way of life. We all agree that this is an outdated way of doing things. We all agree that way of life is out of touch with everyone who want peace and the upholding of the rule of law. This enemy is an enemy of mankind. It is our duty to protect humanity. It is our responsibility to provide collective global justice. And as such we are going to dump all these weapons on his land until not even a small stump is left burning."

"Will that not make us the *Hostis Humani Generis too?*"

"No one can plead ignorance to *Jus Cogens* laws. It's not like someone can misrepresent you because this is common knowledge that these laws can never be broken. The accused has a history of torturing and covering up his tracks. There are no other laws known to mankind that can be used to seek justice. That could explain his complacency and arrogance. All the global institutions have no jurisdiction but thanks to the *Jus Cogens* Laws. The laws that have a universal jurisdiction we can collectively declare war on the enemy. I say we destroy all the things we don't need this way. Evil can only breed evil. There is no sign that the accused will change and stop completely deactivating all dirty tricks. No. It is our human duty to attack. We have a moral obligation as humans to safeguard the existence of humanity. We can only insure this by a complete obliteration. The accused is a serial torturer. Legal precedence has informed us that the torturer has become like the pirates and the slave trader before him. A *Hostis Humanis Generis* and as such I declare war on the accused."

"To Victory! Two Victory!" people started shouting.

"Like I said you shall all surrender all your weapons. From today onward all weapons shall be the property of TWO. Who shall use them according to the new global laws which will be written accordingly. TWO shall pass a new law to outright the making of weapons. We shall move away from defensive economies unless we get visited by aliens. TWO shall outright ban the making of bio-weapons. Instead we shall fund other areas."

"But for centuries the military has created jobs and kept us in power."

"I am not saying stop the military. I am saying with the Inbuilt-Gun we shall never need weapons. TWO shall terminate remotely anyone put on trial and found guilty. Killing shall be the sole duty of TWO.

Every country shall have a representative in TWO."

"What's the differences with today's institutions."

"Today's institutions have become evil cults. Membership is based on geographic regions and is based on differences you must have certain traits to be a member. They have become easily associated with abuse and they defend those who fund them the same people involved in rights abuse. Today's institutions have no powers to pass judgment. They rely on member countries to act, to arrest the accused and that can introduce a bias in the system. With TWO we shall have powers than any leader. We shall not wait for the accused to grow old and frail in the process kill more people needlessly when we can act swiftly. We shall have powers to tackle the issues as soon as. We shall be a global representation of the globe not a bunch or the other wing of the evil and corrupt leaders. We shall be a global force that encourages human development. That encourages superior thinking. We shall declare war on anyone who benefits unfairly at the expense of the fundamental rights of others. We shall be strict on those who don't value women's and children's lives. We shall dedicate our existence to the training of superior assassins to solve global wars. Wars shall be the thing of the past. After this war. There shall never be spending on weapons again at least on the weapons we know today."

"But Mr. President are you talking about World War

Three [WW3]?"

David looked at every one of the leaders.

"Ladies and gentlemen WW3 is what the accused is accounting on. Sacrifice and get more killed. This is his plan and the main reason why he does not stop to torture and torment others. Simply because the odds are stacked in his favor. He abuses, tricks, controls and threatens just about everyone just because he know more will die for him. More will defend him. Evil cults to us but strength in numbers to him. But..."

Everyone looked at him and listened attentively.

"The *Jus Cogens* laws are laws defined as such because they are universal laws that are there to safeguard the existence of humanity. For 2000 years our forefathers were not stupid enough to be involved in acts that will cause human extinction. Take a perfect example, the black death. Millions of humans died. When someone recreates such events, it sends shock-waves through the fabric of human existence. It gives everyone a sense of responsibility to try to stop that person. Imagine what if you end up dead? Let's just say his bio-weapons will kill 50 million people an estimate of the number of people killed by the black death. You will do anything to stop that happening because the odds that you and all the ones you love will die are so unbelievably high and as such you will have a duty to stop the making of the bio-weapons in the first place.

That makes these laws have such a universal jurisdiction. Anyone can act to defend humanity."

Everyone listened nodding their heads.

"A world war is different in the sense that in a world war allies do fight other allied enemies. The notion of *Hostis Humanis Generis* is centered on the fact that no two people in their right minds will commit such a crime. It is a crime that sends shock-waves to the entire system. It's a crime that it's not common for two humans to commit unless if one misrepresent the facts to the other. It is a situation that there will always be two outcomes given that two or more human beings are planning to carry it out. One will always say no this is against humanity unless the other misrepresent the facts. So as such no one will help or defend him without becoming an enemy of mankind. Having said that, we can all be like gangsters and the mob. This is the only way forward with torturers and bio-weapons abusers."

Hudson stood up.

"I will donate 2% of my current military budget to TWO. I am abandoning the bio-weapons plan and investing in other areas like fuel."

"Thank you! That's the spirit Mr. President."

"On top of that I want to be the person to kill this bastard to get even with him for using me for the wrong reasons."

"That's what we want. The world need you Mr. President. Who else?"

Rose stood up.

"I don't have much but I will send my special elite forces whenever needed."

"We can do with any training. A global problem requires a global answer any help is greatly welcome."

People cheered.

"TWO will address the limitations of these institutions. After all, these institutions were created to give protection to the people responsible for the worst crimes. TWO shall eliminate state and individual sovereignty. TWO shall not only prosecute the weak when they are old and frail. We shall prosecute anyone includes the rich and the mighty whether they are still in power or not. We shall be tough with those who are still living in the medieval times. We shall attack with such swiftness and vigor those who are still practicing outdated methods. Who still value stupid ideas formulated in times when oppression and torture were prevalent. We shall promote human development regardless of race, color, religion, gender, sex or social hierarchy. Those who use women and children to push for selfish agendas your time is up."

There was a huge applause as everyone cheered on.

Roxy stood up.

"What is the Inbuilt-Gun?"

"Firstly, I would say that our values are changing and so as our technology. Instead of building weapons spending trillions globally we have been working on this project to enhance human existence and development. Today's leaders have spent trillions reversing previous achievements. Creating methods to reverse everything, making people age faster and younger. Creating new genetically modified-viral agents in order to control and 'REDUCE the VALUE' of competitors and others to gain an unfair competitive advantage. For some few evil ones to blackmail and exterminate others unfairly. They might argue that these tactics are survival tactics, but I say all this should be a thing of the past. We have spent $millions looking for ways to eliminate aging. We are aiming to prolong life. The idea is to find better alternatives and improve humanity."

"But Inbuilt-Gun suggest more than just an ordinarily gun."

"Yes. First let me point out that, we embarked on this program to eliminate all things being reversed by the current government, aging, a high rate of birth defects, high disability rates for a developed country, and high infertility among others. We have encouraged the better valuing of human life. Having said that, we will spend money you would otherwise have used on weapons to develop high intelligent gadgets that help human existence and developments.

These gadgets will foster human development. These gadgets will form part of the human development process. We will encourage everyone to have the gadgets as a way of protecting everyone."

"You said an Inbuilt-Gun?"

"Whenever someone commits a crime, the person will be brought to justice and if found guilty, the gadget will be used to kill the person. The Inbuilt-Gun. Meaning it's a good device to protect you but one that can be converted once it is found out that you are guilty."

"It sounds like the ones everyone has already. The medical devices the IMDs,"

"The ones you have were built to reverse all previous achievements. They are used to control you so that you obey without resisting. They are tools of oppression used to blackmail you. Used to 'Reduce your Value'. Used to leave 'watermarks' on you to guarantee you as theirs, their objects which they can easily use. The current IMDs are used to enslave you, to make you cheaper so that you obey and follow commands. They are there to track, monitor and spy on you. Whereas the ones I am advocating for are there to serve you. You are the driver you have all the priorities, you can command them and not someone else. These are best secured and can't be hacked. All the trillions being spent on weapons should be used on these to eliminate aging, to eliminate all diseases, not to be used for torture, or for the loading of man-made bio-threats. If pollution increases, these will help purify the air internally. With these they will be mandatory as the benefits will outweigh anything else. Instead of waging wars any disputes will be resolved in global courts that represent the globe not just the few and rich. If found guilty, the gadget becomes an inbuilt-gun. No need for weapons. All issues settled in the global courts. No more unnecessary wars killing women and children. A superior humanity a move away from defensive thinking. The world will become a just society again. That eliminates differences. Any disputes will be settled peacefully."

"It seems you are just taking over from the accused. Is that so?"

"Let me make it clear that the accused 's motives are to blackmail you. Today's IMDs are there to enslave you. They give the current government a competitive advantage as they can easily spy on you. The ones I am proposing are there to serve you. You are the master for a change. You command it to do what you like it to do. Look around you. I challenge you today. Travel anywhere and count how many people you meet today with all kinds of issues. People you think they have aged badly that it's unbelievable, etc. We will destroy evil. No one will ever use this to cause disabilities, to discourage miscegenation therefore the dilution of his people. No one shall use the gadgets to blackmail you whenever you have money in your bank so that you give them the money. All these evil people will never be in our world. Evil can only breed evil. Like I said earlier on we shall aim together for a total annihilation. Let's work together. The Inbuilt-Gun will act as a deterrent so that everyone will obey the rule of law and uphold it and for the few unlucky ones, we shall deliver justice that way."

She paused for a while.

"The accused has used this Inbuilt-Gun to assassinate our leaders before because they stood up against the making of bio-weapons. Let us not forget that our President Brian was a good President. The only crime he committed was standing against evil cults. Denouncing those who reversed previous achievements. Denounced those who were making bio-weapons to kill many in order to harvest organs. Denounced those who brought terror to others so that they gain unfairly things such as goods, money and skilled people. It is daylight robbery. President Brian condemned secret torture. He condemned it's use as a way of guaranteeing control of the people. The inbuilt-Gun was used to kill him. This theory explains all the facts that were not coherent with the circumstances and the evidence at hand.

CHAPTER ELEVEN

Kayden wiped the sweat droplets from his forehead. He looked at the United Nations Security Council judges. He walked to the middle of the preliminary hearing room. They all looked at him.

"Mr. Kayden. You are asking us to believe your story without any proof or tangible evidence don't you think you are asking too much from us."

Kayden remained silent.

"I am telling you that they are committing genocide. I am the proof that they are exterminating thousands to harvest organs. They are making bio-weapons and using these to kill people in order to harvest organs."

The judges smiled for a while and looked at Mr. Kayden.

"Do you see how we are finding it hard to believe your story. You are standing here, and you are trying to convince us that you have a heart of one of the victims. If that was true you could be dead by now. I checked your medical records and there is totally nothing wrong with you. We also believe that people in your situation would react the way you are reacting,"

"You have to believe me."

"Mr. Kayden it's not that they might have got you a heart of someone who was murdered but that could be just circumstantial."

Kayden stopped and looked behind him. Paige got up and held the hand of a boy and walked to the center of the preliminary court.

"I have someone I want you to meet."

"Don't worry tell them what you just told me." said Paige.

The boy looked at everyone and then at Paige.

"Don't be shy. It's okay. Tell them."

"They murdered my father. They killed my daddy."

Everyone looked at him.

"Who killed your daddy?"

"The dangerous men."

"What do these men look like?"

The boy remained quiet for a while before looking at Paige.

"It's okay. Show them."

The boy walked to the desk and took out his drawing. He walked to the judge and gave him the drawing. The judge looked at the drawing for a while.

"Okay thank you." said the judge before the boy walked back to his seat and sat down.

"Mr. Kayden. Okay, I will give you the chance to explain yourself."

"Thank you, your honor."

"The accused has become very devious and manipulating. Somehow, he has found a way of robbing rich foreigners that settle in his country. Once you in you can't take anything out but you don't get told any of these before you settle. My problems started after settling. I started sending money out to my son. I bought a new company and moved houses and cities that meant changing my doctor too. New registration, routines checks and all that stuff. I went for a minor operation to screen for genetics etc. Months later maybe, seven, I started vibrating."

He looked at everyone and then at his wife.

"One day at work. I heard a familiar voice while in my office. I got up but somehow, I lost my sight even though my eyes were opened. I discovered that they had implanted something that blinds eyes pulling the iris to the side so that vision is lost. The man whose voice I heard was the operating doctor. He placed a knife on my heart and suggested I needed a new heart. I had to donate money to a certain charity. I declined. I was in perfect health. That time I was sending money abroad as you know I came with $billions. The more I sent money out the more my heart beat changed positions."

"Changed positions?"

"Yes, your honor. I started feeling my heart beat anywhere, stomach, private parts, legs everywhere. I later found out that they were stopping my heart swapping it with an IMD of some kind. The IMD was used to hack my system."

"Your honor. The reason Mr. Kayden came to ask for my client's help was because he had these problems in the first place."

"Let him finish."

"As I was saying, I ended up donating the money. The mistake I did as things got worse. The doctor further threatened that unless I get a new heart thing were never going to be the same again. I found out that all the time I would feel a heartbeat in different organs they were weakening my otherwise good heart. The heart normally should pump blood continuously throughout one's life, but they alternated it with this IMD. In the end my own heart was weak that now I needed the transplant. They used the IMD to control sexual functions as well. Speaking of abuse and evil. In the end I had a transplant after donating money again. They had threatened my son abroad, so I agreed. Months later we started seeing a boy outside our house. On further investigation we found out that he was the son of the woman whose heart I had. At that time, we had threatened to expose them then they threatened us more. They admitted of killing these people to harvest body parts to meet their long organ waiting list shortage. The only way to do that was to release a bio-weapon. That way they can harvest organs in the name of research and that way no one suspects their organ harvesting activities. They said this also assures them that I will keep my mouth shut. If I don't, they can use the IMD to kill me and blame it on the victim's donated heart."

There was silence.

"IMD used to kill and create the symptoms?"

"A device implanted on the lumbar is operated just like a drone remotely to produce electric that is used to stimulate nerves. The device [IMD] is used to produce the same effects for it has a propeller that rotates shaking body parts to induce any movements."

"So, you are saying that this device creates same symptom as the real bio-weapon?"

"Yes. The vibrations cause the nerves to imitate the symptoms."

Kayden stopped and looked at everyone.

"Over the years I have discovered that this device is like a CD player, a radio cassette, a small computer. Such as that it relies on external commands that are delivered remotely. Just like a CD player that requires a Cd to function or like a cassette player that requires a cassette this device requires external input to function. The device is also like a computer that requires a software input. They have developed digital software this is where it makes sense. They are making digital versions of bio-weapons, a software they are using to load the device."

"Wait, a minute. A digital software version with a signature of a real bio-weapon?"

"Exactly your honor. This software is loaded remotely just like a drone. Most important, they have loaded their people with attacking software."

"Mr. Kayden who will believe that."

"Let me explain. Everyone is armed with these devices disguised as medical records or small personal computer. What most don't know is that they have repellent software. This works the same as watermarks. Don't forget the accused is a strong supporter of eugenics principles toned done to patriotic values. Having said that every one of them is armed with this repellent software."

"So, you are saying these people are loaded with the digital versions to bio-weapons?"

"Precisely each and everyone has a signature different to each other. For most they act only as watermarks to repel or protect them to prevent the miscegenation and degeneration of their people. This is local. But it's a different story when they got to hunt and harvest abroad for organs. They launch the lethal digital versions. These actually kill."

"Your honor this is nonsense losing an organ can make one hallucinate just like Mr. Kayden here. Who on earth would even think of harvesting victims of such an epidemic?"

"Extermination and large-scale organs harvesting disguised as an epidemic, so no one will even question their motives. This explains also why the other research team did not find any biologicals presence."

"This is nonsense your honor."

"It does not stop there they are trafficking the kids of the victims. They then implant these IMD's as well turning these into slaves throughout their life. Grooming and using these as prostitutes before killing them and harvesting organs as well."

"I would not put any weight to that."

"Your honor if they can do this to me what stops them to do the same to an orphaned kid. If they can kill abroad in broad-daylight. Harvesting body organs, what can stop them doing the same in their country?"

"Your honor a single event cannot be said to represent a common widespread and systematic event."

"This is just the tip of the ice-berg. A single incident can reflect the wider practice especially if we look at their political views that are still rooted in the eugenics ideas you can come to the same conclusion as me that the accused is an enemy of mankind involved in genocide, torture and organ harvesting among others.”

He looked at everyone.

David got off his Presidential limousine and entered the conference hall. A lot of people had gathered inside.

“TWO victory! TWO victory!”

“Our Future! Our Say!”

“Your Future Your Say!”

“Ladies and gentlemen today if an important day in the history of mankind. We have consulted with everyone else. Surprising there are still some people among us who are advocating for a Do-nothing approach.”

Some people clapped hands and cheered on.

“Human mentality is wired such that when there is no tremendous change then they will tend to do the same thing. This is true. We only react to things that shock us. Things that brings in fear. Things that changes the way we think. If we look throughout history changes has only been achieved when drastic measures are taken. Human mind is wired so that when no one reacts that means whatever one is doing is accepted or people don’t see the need for change. This is true. I don’t want to make the same mistake as our forefather Duncan.”

People clapped hands.

"We cannot make the same mistake as Duncan."

He stopped and looked at everyone.

"Duncan had the opportunity to set things rights. Duncan had an opportunity to pave the way for a new beginning. Duncan had the moral duty to act for the sake of humanity. Duncan had the big opportunity to prepare the way for everyone. To lay the foundation but..."

Everyone looked at him.

"But he chose fame and neglected his duty to mankind to put the record straight."

He paused.

"Duncan is regarded a hero by many, but I ask you this? Hero to who and for what? We as humans we have moral obligations and duties to safeguard humanity. But Duncan chose to ignore his duty. Ladies and gentlemen, we cannot afford to make that mistake. We cannot afford to make such a stupid mistake! Had he acted today we could be in a better position. Had he acted we could have seen a change. Had he acted Delaney could have stopped. Had he acted he could have laid the foundation. A foundation for everyone not just us but our kids and their kids as well. Had he acted we could be in a better position to bargain. So, having said that I say doing nothing is worse. Change, ladies and gentlemen will never come easily. Doing nothing simply encourages Delaney to carry on doing what we are saying are outdated methods out of touch with today's reality. Correct me if I am wrong. There is no change in history that came when nothing was done. We do the things we are doing because we see the benefits. Delaney today is still torturing people. Still using bio-weapons and digital versions to exterminate people. I don't care why he does it. population control, shortage of organs and a long waiting list, to safeguard the existence and continuous existence of his people, etc. I say we cannot let that continue to happen. What he has done is becoming even more devious and secretive. He has devised new torture methods, he has developed digital versions of bio-weapons and somehow made devices like small computers that he loads with digital-viral weapons that he is using to kill, harvest organs, kidnap orphans whom he then gives to his clients for them to abuse. So, to all those who are advocating for a Do-nothing solution I say think again. If you were Delaney and if nothing is done would you change?"

He looked at everyone.

"Ladies and gentlemen doing nothing when it comes to *Jus Cogens* laws is a crime. What I want all of you to understand today is that we have laws. Laws that were written to ensure the existence of humanity. If you say we do nothing when it's a law that requires action, then something is wrong. That threatens the fabric in which our society was founded. People have died for lesser causes so that we have the freedoms we have today. I would advise you all that Duncan although he is presented as our hero the fact that he chose to do nothing erased all his good acts in a flash. I don't want that stigma on myself, my kids and their kids. These laws exonerate anyone who acts to preserve humanity. We all have a moral duty to fulfill Delaney's wishes. The moment he tortured, the moment he committed genocide and the moment he killed to harvest organs Delaney signed his own death certificate. These laws are to be taken seriously and acted upon. Having said that, I say it is human nature not to change. Some people will never change. This is deep seated in their bones that we must act hence these laws. To start a new beginning, we must eliminate the bad people. I can't guarantee anyone that they will change, and I am not Duncan and would not take chances. Having said that, I would say doing nothing violates human existence notions. Doing nothing simply perpetuate evil. We cannot wait until Delaney is ousted and old. We can't let others suffer on our watch. TWO has authority and powers to remove state immunity the way it should be. TWO have powers to pass judgment and punishment and as the President of TWO I say we attack swiftly without any negotiations."

There was a huge buzz.

"We all know that Delaney is evil there is no doubt. He only pretended to help only because he was exposed. We know it's a fact he is still torturing people. We also know why he is doing it. He still has the sense of security once provided by all the institutions he established to give him immunity and an alibi. He is looking to World War 3. He is expecting everyone to join him and die for him. I say I would not die for him nor do I expect anyone to die for him too. Let's not forget that his acts are acts that will cause the extinction of humanity. Such crimes have universal jurisdiction, and everyone has a duty to pass judgment. I say we warn his people. We let them choose. Run away or die with your leader. Evil can only breed evil. If they stand by him, then they die by him too."

The people started clapping hands and applauding.

"We have achieved great over the centuries. People have fought and died for us to have what we have today. The dreams for all those who died were to take humanity to the next level of advancement as nature intended. Unfortunately, some have forsaken all that and are taking us back to the time we had nothing. The time we were ravaged with all kinds of problems. We cannot let that happen! We have rights and obligations to preserve and advance humanity. Unfortunately, some have chosen the evil road, but I stand here today and declare war to them. We shall attack like a wild fire from all corners of the earth until there is not even a burning stump left."

There was a huge row.

"It shall not stop there. We shall search and hunt all the people involved in this mess. I mean all of them and execute judgment swiftly. We shall destroy each and everyone involved knowingly and unknowingly. We cannot accept excuses for such a crime. No one shall plead ignorance as a defense. A list of all involved will be posted on the internet and everywhere and I repeat you all have a moral duty to preserve humanity. You all have a moral obligation to act. Doing nothing is a crime for you will become like them. Everyone has a duty to humanity to capture and put on trial these perpetrators of justice and execute them. We need a new beginning and it can only come if we eliminate all these evil people."

"TWO victory! TWO victory!

"Our Future! Our Say!"

CHAPTER TWELVE

Delaney looked at his wife.

"How can you say that? How on earth will I preserve our way of life? How will I be able to protect you my love?"

"At least we will be together. Your support has changed drastically. I don't feel the love of the people anymore. Just leave all this. Life is changing. You are destroying our people. If they attack do you think they will spare us?"

Delaney looked at his wife.

"You don't understand that will be giving up thousand years of history do you know what that means? Do you have any idea of the stigma that will be on our kids?"

"Delaney it does matter. At least stop this project before things get out of hand. Move with the times. This eugenics notion is out of date with reality."

"I can't give up all this. Don't be scared. No one can predict the outcome of a war. It can go anywhere."

His wife walked to the bed and sat down.

"I have spent $millions getting support all I just need is a call for help."

"Who will support you?"

"Who? You are asking me who? Everyone."

His wife lay down on the bed.

"They explained your crimes. They are calling you a *Hostis Humanis Generis*. Do you know what that means?"

"They can call me anything they like. Do I care? In fact, I was once called a devil, and that's worse I think."

"They said that every human being has a moral duty to preserve humanity."

She looked at him. He could see the glittering in her eyes.

"I have a duty to preserve our people."

Lily lay down tears trickling down the ridge between her eyes.

"How did it get to this? You are over doing it. They are humans too. You treat them like they are pieces of meat."

Delaney opened his eyes wide open. He fumed with rage.

"You forgot already, huh?"

She did not say anything.

"You forget the Black death?"

"What does that have to do with what is happening?"

"I am not taking chances. We nearly got wiped out. I have a duty to preserve my people if that means killing all so be it. I am just doing my job. If you were in my position, you would understand."

"It's you actually making all these bio-weapons. It's you shooting yourself in the foot."

"Everyone has an antidote. If they touch my people, it's at their own risk. I gave them houses to live. I gave them food and clothing. The only thing I asked was not to dilute my people."

"But you are causing all these problems. They don't call you an enemy of mankind for nothing. If they attack how are you going to protect the people? Do you think they will leave anyone alive especially knowing that you have loaded everyone with these genetically modified watermarks as you call them?"

Delaney stopped and looked at her.

"How do they know that?"

Lily sat on the bed and looked at Delaney.

"People were disappearing you didn't hear."

"No one tell me anything nowadays. These ungrateful cunts. I work very hard putting myself at risk to protect them and this is what I get?"

"You spent all money over these years making watermarks when people were starving. Some now say all this money should have been used to advance your people's way of life."

Delaney picked up a glass and threw it against the wall.

"Ungrateful cunts! Now you talk nonsense. How can I preserve our people without embarking on such a project? They can't touch anyone without falling sick that's protection. No dilution or degeneration of our elite genes with inferior genes."

"Did the people you are talking about found?"

"Yes, most returned, but they had their computers removed."

"Removed? By whom?"

She lay back on the bed.

"Now I understand why they are calling me that name. Get everyone right now. I want all the leaders summoned immediately."

For the first time Delaney wore a haunted face. For the first time fear was written all over his face.

Imogen entered the laboratory at TWO headquarters.

"We can't get an antidote to the digital version of the weapon. It's some complicated code and we can't break it. We advised the people to stay away from computers and anything that transmit rays that are fired remotely."

"What are you saying?"

"They are firing these digital agents remotely and instantly becomes part of that device."

"What is the worst scenario?"

"If we can't break the code, I am afraid we have no use of his people?"

"What is that supposed to mean?"

"They have 'personal computers' if programmed will attack all others with different digital numbers."

"They are all weapons as well?"

"Exactly! No wonder why so many people died. The worst thing is that his people don't know that themselves."

"Are you saying that none of our men can break this code?"

She shook her head.

"Get me the Head of Defense and the Weapons Specialist Commander."

"Already done. Conference call."

David looked at the screen.

"I didn't know that it's this complicated."

The two men on the screens looked down for a while.

"We just received the findings of the eight years

investigation report and it does not look good."

"I am listening."

"I would like to say that he might have shot himself in the head."

"Is that bad?"

"Somehow in the process to preserve his people he might have actually created a time bomb."

"In other words what Mark is saying is that the watermarks have become weapons, and it's a mistake waiting to happen. I understand the scientist were commissioned by President Hudson."

"Meaning?"

"Hudson is working on him."

"Hudson" he whispered.

"So are you saying we just sit but for how long."

"No sitting Sir. I am just saying that it's total obliteration. Watermarks will become weapons."

"Antidotes?"

"If he can afford to pay the scientist?"

"Do they need to get paid I thought?"

"Hudson's plan I think it's better if you talk to him."
"Okay get him on the line."

David walked up and down before a crackling sound startled him.

"Yes Mr. President."

"He thought he was clever sending me to a meaningless war to kill women and children just to cover his evil deeds what else did you expect."

"We are in the process of asking people to evacuate..."

"Mr. President evacuate? I don't think so. They are all corrupt. Each one of them."

"Antidote. Will the scientists be able to provide one as soon as possible?"

"Mr. President you don't get it. They are all now corrupted. The scientist's demands for huge sums before providing antidotes are just time delaying tactics. I got the approval of the leaders before TWO took over."

"Obliteration?"

"Until there is not even a smoldering stump left. Even if we wanted, it will be exposing our pure people to all kinds of watermarks and to be honest we don't know what's in the watermarks. We can't take risks Delaney have developed a sophisticated digital attacking warfare that has never been witnessed before. Each one is a digital-soldier capable of attacking remotely knowing or unknowingly. Mr. President are you prepared and equipped to deal with these humans turned digital-soldiers?"

"If we can talk to Delaney first...."

"We reached a judgment already. No time for negotiations. The G-clamp plan is ready. We shall attack from all corners of the earth swiftly and precisely.

"The G-clamp plan?" repeated David.

"Yes Sir. You know the drill. We have already programmed the reverse or U-turn impact. When they attack with their digital-soldiers, that will cause the destruction of their own antidote thereby committing suicide. But we have to set all on fire as well to protect our own?"
"Does Delaney know all this?"

"If he knows then tomorrow someone might cry genocide Mr. President. We just flatten the land."

Years later

Eve walked to her father and handed him a book.

"Is that you daddy?"

David smiled.

"Let me tell you a story. Once in a world far away. The President of one country was very concerned about preserving his country and his people that he spent all the country's money preserving his way of life. Little did he know that his people were struggling. Poverty was widespread. This President would collect money from everyone and send it to make stronger and stronger viral agents and use these as watermarks so that his people remained pure untouched by the foreigners. He had promised his father that he was going to protect their way of life. In order to protect his people, he started forcing sterilization, making viral agents and using these on foreigners so that they won't touch his people and have kids with them. There is a time when there was an uprising but that only saw more and more injustice. To defend himself and avoid claims of abuse he started illegally operating on everyone implanting whatever he can if his people were undiluted, he didn't care. Year after year he developed stronger and stronger watermarks that in the end his people were the ones now contaminated that everyone was running away from them. The watermarks were permanent and required huge sums to be removed. He would order the destruction of anyone until one day there was a rise to power of a new global political group that changed everything."

"So, what happened to him and his people? Where are they now?"

"They were all eaten by the sharks."

"Really oh I feel sorry for them."

"No one wanted to be with them they had dangerous watermarks they would shoot everyone. He expected a war, but dad had other plans."

"Were they thrown in the ocean?"

"They jumped into the ocean and they were all swept away."

"But daddy I heard stories that they are still living down the ocean waters."

"They say some few good ones still live there."

"Why they don't come out up here? Is it true that they only come out at night?"

David smiled.

"The weather changed, and it was cold everywhere that most died. The land was covered in oceanic water. The watermarks attracted a lot of sharks that most were eaten alive. The few that survived remained underneath the water. They only come out at night when sharks are in deep oceans."

"Is that why mummy always go out at night?"

"David stop lying to your daughter. Eve your daddy blew up all our people including your grand-mum and grandpa."

"Do you go out at night to look for them?"

She hugged her daughter.

"Yes, my beautiful. I go out to look for your grandparents and my sister."

"Why you blew up my grandparents?"

Eve folded her lips and looked upset.

"They all had become scary zombies."

She looked at her mum and relaxed.

"But mum is beautiful."

She looked at her mum. David's wife looked at him.

"I love you. But I am still mad you should have done something. The most powerful man in the world and you still can't save my parents?"

"In politics double standards can get you shot."

"Double standard my ass! What am I still doing here?"

"You are exceptionally beautiful. You listened to me."

"I can say the same about my parents you know."

"I thought you said you are from Russia. See what happens when you lie to me? Come here right now." David chased after his wife and kid. They all run away laughing.

Hudson stood in his office looking at the big screen.

He kicked the air. He paced left and down.

"I don't like it when people lie to me. Get him on the phone right now."

"Daddy it's yours." said Eve handing the phone to her father.

"Do you know why I destroyed Delaney and his people? He misrepresented the facts and what on earth do you think you are doing?"

"My mission completed. Thank you for letting me take your position. Let's just say for delegating to me."

"What? Are you saying...?"

"Yes Mr. President. I have no use for this role. I guess you have cleaned your hands. You have restored your trust. And I am confident that you will make a good global President. Sir."

"I thought this is what you wanted. To be the leader and President of TWO?"

"Speaking of which..."

Instantly his wife and kid appeared on the screen.

"I don't like it when people lie to me. Come here right now," shouted David chasing after his wife and kid.

David's wife and kid runaway.

"Sorry Sir. She told me she was from Latvia?"

Hudson sat down and smiled before pausing the screen.

CHAPTER THIRTEEN

David, Brody, Antony, Joyclene, Chelsea, Timothy, Nancy and Shyleen entered the TWO presidential building. They walked to the conference hall. There were many guests attending the President's ballroom. Julia approached them with a tray with champagne glasses.

"Ladies and gentlemen. On behalf of the President we welcome you. Champagne?"

The men and women took glasses of champagne and walked to the front of the hall. There were so many people elegantly dressed. Everyone chatting to each other. David and Chelsea walked toward the President who was busy talking to other guests.

"Mr. President."

"Mr. Vice President. Welcome please."

He stretched his hand toward his office. The Vice President David, Chelsea and Hudson entered the office.

"I am glad everything went according to plan."

"Wasn't sure we could flatten it that quickly."

"Speaking of which..."

The President opened his laptop and turned it facing David and Chelsea.

"$700trillion?"

"Electronic transfer that I just received."

"Much needed funds. It's not easy to be the President of TWO. A global leader, surely this money will come in handy."

"Great idea to flatten the land render it obsolete and get the electronic transfer."

"Not just that Mr. President. We did the world a favor. Away with evil."

"I just can't believe why some people can't go with the flow and move with the times. Delaney was an embarrassment."

"No regrets. How could we have moved forward when he was stuck in the medieval times?"

"Thanks to the electronic transfer system we rendered that country obsolete. Flatten the land and get a wire transfer. We have peace in the world, we have money in the bank and a lot of space not mentioning a lot breath of fresh air."

David walked closer to Hudson.

"We might actually need to render another country obsolete soon. Flatten the land and get an electronic transfer."

Chelsea looked at him.

"What are you talking about?" asked the President Hudson.

David looked at Chelsea with a face that seemed to say please excuse us. Instantly Chelsea got the idea.

"Excuse me I will check on the other gentlemen."

David waited for Chelsea to leave the office.

"Someone powered on Delaney's computer."

"Impossible," replied Hudson sitting in his sofa.

"I thought so at first then again I realized that we might still have an enemy within."

Hudson breathed heavily.

"Is that why Delaney was so cocky and arrogant?"

"I think so. I glad, I was right after all that we avoid a world war but simply individual onslaught."

"How bad is it?"

"Very bad I would say."

David sat down as well.

"How can we preach of change of advancing humanity? Advocating for the superior thinking when we can't even free ourselves. How can a leader purport to change the way people think? How can a leader change people's attitude when he is just a puppet? A person who can't make his own decision.

A person still oppressed himself."

"But Delaney is gone so I don't see any problem."

"That's not the issue. Although he is a President, he is also a spy."

"But he doesn't know that?"

"I know that's why I am saying let's just make his land obsolete and get the electronic transfer."

Hudson stood up and walked to the window.

"That sounds harsh especially the fact that he has no idea that Delaney did this to him."

"I know but life is not fair you know. He is technically leaking all information. I guess Delaney's buddy is still among us."

"How can we speak of advancing humanity when we are still entangled in a web of subordination? A puppet is just like a slave. Worse if it's a President. What message does that send to the people? You are preaching of uplifting humanity when you are suppressed yourself."

"There is something we can do. I guess there are still at least two more countries we can render obsolete and get a transfer."

"Wait, a minute. If we start doing it to others that might make us look bad. Don't forget I worked hard to reestablish myself. I don't want any more controversy."

"But Mr. President. You know the protocol. We have at least two spies."

"I know Mr. Vice President, but I am saying that we have to come up with a plan."

"I have a plan already. You know how we handle spies. Make it a public affair. Shock and shame. Then go after the puppet master."

"But Delaney is dead."

"There must be someone else. It's a mockery of our global party."

"Mr. Vice President. I know but I am saying that if you were in his or her shoes, would you not find this to be unfair?"

There was a moment of silence.

"I know but protocol tells us exactly what to do. To deter others, we must adopt the shock and shame tactic. We can't tolerate Trojan horses. We don't what to be a laughingstock. We dealt perfectly with Delaney we should clean all mess straight away."

The two men sipped their champagne before a beep sound startled both. Hudson looked at David and then at the laptop. He reached for the laptop and flipped open the top flap. He quickly read the message and looked at David.

"You are okay? You look like you have seen a ghost Mr. President?"

Hudson did not reply straight away he looked lost in thoughts.

"I am okay just my reminder I have to do something later on."

"I think everything is going according to plan. We have enough money to solve all global issues."

"Mr. Vice President we will never solve all the problems, but we can do what we can."

"You sound like you are giving up Mr. President you don't sound so convincing."

"$700trillion just not enough."

"I know."

"You know Mr. Vice President?"

"Yes Mr. President. That's why I am saying that we should render at least two more countries obsolete. We can always get an electronic transfer."

"Mr. Vice President. I told you that I have a reputation to keep. I suggest this time we just deal with the individuals blowing up everyone might not be a good idea. How will we justify that? It was easy with Delaney and his people. Everyone knew they were crooked."

"We follow protocol then. We eliminate these last two."

"What do we know about the subject?"

"His name is Mr. Kayden. He lived abroad for some

time before bad things started happening. He lodged a lawsuit that was thrown out, but little did he know that Delaney had tampered with him. Spying and putting a surveillance on him. Ever since he had return and became President. All these years Delaney was getting an unfair advantage listening to all his conversations and using these against him. Blackmailing him and releasing private information until he did what he wanted."

"Is that why there were assassination attempts on him?"

"I think some knew he was nothing than a Trojan for Delaney."

"What happened to the lawsuit?"

"I understand they blackmailed him."

There was a moment of silence.

"He has a son with his estranged wife."

"Oh, I see. Who tried to assassinate him?"

David sat up straight.

"National security guys."

David leaned forward.

"Inside job?"

"Don't you think it's an embarrassment to national security and all special forces when your President is nothing than a Trojan horse. A spy for your enemy. That's an embarrassment to national security and all the things we stand for. No wonder the security guys wanted to take him down. An inside job. They had adopted a shock and shame tactic to send a powerful message."

"The assassination attempts an inside job?"

"To be able to protect the country they had to protect it from the President first. I guess someone just saw no sense in all this and tried to take him down,"

"Holy Sugar! It's more complicated than I thought."

"I guess these guys tried to follow protocol when dealing with a spy. Now you see why I fought to get rid of Delaney."

"Good job Mr. Vice President."

"They did something abroad to him. Hacked him."

"But I understand he had a medical procedure maybe he needed the operation."

"He never needed that thing or the new heart. That was Delaney's trade mark. He would abuse you then sell to you something you don't need. If you refuse, then he damages the good organ until you needed a new one in the end. That explains the lawsuits. Delaney was evil let me tell you this Mr. President. The whole world had succumbed to his dirty tricks. He targeted rich fathers with their sons. Threaten to kill their son until he ended up doing want, he was asked to do."

Colin stormed out of the office. Derek followed him.

He stopped and puffed his electric cigarette.

"That motherfucker can't tell me what to do."

"Calm down he is your boss. You have to do what he asks you to do."

Colin blew the smoke up.

"My boss? Are fucking mad? That spy telling me how to solve my cases who does he think he is? I think I need to solve him first. Don't you think it's an embarrassment? All these crooks are now telling me to get lost just because of him."

"Let those responsible deal with him. You just do your job okay."

"My job is to put a bullet in all these crooks but how can I do that when the biggest crook is our boss?"

"I don't think he has a clue. He got abused abroad."

"Not our fault. I tried to tell him. How many times did I tell him that I don't take orders from him?"

"He thinks you are just being stubborn."

"I am sacred for myself. I got out there who ever did this to him is leaking information. That puts me at risk too."

"It should be safe. Delaney is dead."

"I don't think it was just Delaney."

He looked at Derek.

"What do you mean?"

"Just this morning something came on my radar. If Delaney is dead so who is still trying to communicate with him?"

Paige opened the door and walked to the window.

"I thought the death of Delaney would bring us some peace and some sense of resolve."

Kayden got up and hugged his wife.

"Off course my dear it did. To be honest, I don't what to talk about the past. Why dwell in the past when we have all this life ahead of us?"

"I thought so too but this morning I had a tip."

She turned around and looked at Kayden straight in his eyes.

"What are you talking about?"

"I had a tip that they might try to do to us like what they did to Delaney."

"You must be joking. Right?"

"No. They might have dug our past."

"I lodged a lawsuit that is enough after all these courts archived my files for at least a year but most up to ten years. Trust me there is nothing to worry about."

"I am sacred. If they know. I understand they shoot in broad light any spies. Delaney might have set us up too. How do these people know what happens in our bedroom?"

"Trust me whatever reason they might attack us for that has nothing to do with what happened to me."

"How can you be so sure?"

"My love that's how we make money. Do you think they just obliterated Delaney's country simply because he was a bad person?"

"That's what everyone is saying."

"I know but there is a monetary value as well. I tell you a story my father once told me. Long before there was the electronic money there was gold and all kinds of bank bills. On 11 September 1853 there was the first electronic telegraph system that rendered what was once the financial focal point obsolete. This was the old system, but they needed a new system which was made possible by the first use of the electronic telegraph system. There was no need for the Telegraph Hill building that housed all paperwork of securities regarding the merchant exchange. To move to the new system with immediate effect, they had to destroy the old system. Write everything off and get insurance money for it before installing or starting the new system. That automatically render the Telegraph Hill buildings obsolete. A new beginning and a new start. A new electronic money system then replaced the old system."

"Kayden my love are you suggesting that they deliberately destroyed Delaney's country for the money transfer."

"Yes, on top of Delaney being the devil of-course. For whatever decision all these President's take there is always a monetary value. Do you know how much they received as electronic money transfer when they rendered his country obsolete?"

"It's underwater what good is that to anyone?"

"Now but before they attacked it was valued at $700 trillion just the land without considering artifacts and possessions Delaney stole over the years."

"So, are you saying that they are calling us spies so that they trade the land and us for an electronic transfer in the form of insurance?"

"Protocol but like I said I lodged a lawsuit that I am not a spy I am a victim."

"So, what do they do to spies then?"

Kayden looked down for a while.

"You don't need to know that. It doesn't matter we are safe my love."

"Okay but tell me. I don't want any surprises."

Kayden looked like he had seen a ghost. For the first time he realized that danger was real. He had been briefed repeatedly about the protocol. He looked at his wife and walked toward her and hugged her.

"So, are you going to tell me or not?"

CHAPTER FOURTEEN

Hudson stood up and walked in the conference hall. He stopped and looked at everyone.

"We worked hard and sacrificed a lot to build a better world for us and everyone else. We made it a mandate to maintain peace and order and advance human development through policies that utilizes resources for the better of mankind. Delaney was out of touch with reality. Delaney was a disease himself. We had to do something about it. We were compelled to act which we did in swiftness. I believe that all of you agree with me that the world is a better place without Delaney."

They all agreed and clapped hands.

"TWO victory! TWO victory!"

"I think it will be a big mistake if some of us still admire Delaney and all his crooked ways."

He stood up and looked at David and everyone else.

"Some people never change. Taking Delaney for example. We did what is humanly possible to try to resolve this peacefully, but Delaney wouldn't listen. No matter how many times we advised him he was so sure that his was the best way. He sabotaged everything we stand for. Believe you me when I say we want to work together with everyone here to advance humanity. To change our ways for the better."

He stopped and walked in front of everyone.

"Sabotaging all our efforts would be a big mistake. We build our globe the way we want it and we cannot allow people who will try to sabotage our efforts."

There was a huge buzz.

"Yes, I believe someone here is still in Delaney's world. Someone here still think like Delaney. Sabotaging everything beautiful and render it useless. Long time ago. When I was still the President of my country, I bought two precious diamonds of equal size and value. I gave one to Delaney to keep for me. The other I gave to my friend Chelsea over there."

Chelsea lifted her hand.

"After one year I went to Chelsea and requested my diamond back."

He looked at her and smiled.

"She took me to this big hall in the city center. On my way there I was thinking out loud that hey what the fuck? I expected her to keep it on herself may be attached to her bra or something."

They are laughed.

"Never mind. I arrived there and could not enter at first. There were so many people who had come to see and ogle the diamond. Guess what it was in a glass cabinet that was secure thanks for that. Ladies and gentlemen, the diamond had made me more money. It was well polished everyone wanted to have a selfie with it. I looked at Chelsea and fumed. I gave her thinking that she will treat it like my heart. My heart being shared by all those people that's disgusting, I thought."

Everyone laughed.

"After everyone had gone, she took a key from the pocket in her knickers."

Everyone laughed.

"She opened the cabinet and retrieved the diamond and caressed it kissing it. Then I smiled as she handed it to me. 'To all the visitors, for their eyes only but to me the intimacy is out of this world,' she claimed. I nodded my head in appreciation. She showed me on the internet how famous the diamond had become worldwide without anyone touching it. Hours after that I received phone calls. She had told everyone that the owner was back and would sell the diamond if the offer was right."

They clapped hands, and she stood up and opened her hands kneeling before sitting down.

"The next day I flew to Delaney's country. I was very excited. I thought I could experience another magic time like the one Chelsea had given me. Delaney was not even bothered. He offered me a beer and told me to relax and sit-down."

They all laughed.

"Trust me, I love beer but this day I didn't want anything to do with beer. The moment he looked away I threw the beer on the couch. I am thinking that okay maybe now he will give me back my diamond. In my mind I started thinking that maybe he sold it and he is sacred to tell me. But we all know Delaney was very rich. I thought that maybe someone had stolen it. Okay if that's the case no problem I had it insured. The insurance woman who had volunteered to accompany me to collect the second one started getting worried. So, I gathered my courage and asked him to give me back my diamond without delay. Do you know what he said?"

"No," they all shouted.

"He said don't worry it's in a safe place. Relax no one will steal it."

He paused.

"I relaxed and looked straight toward his beautiful mansion. In my mind I was hoping that he had displayed the diamond in a golden glass cabinet for only his rich friends to ogle. I looked at the insurance woman and pointed to the big mansion with my eyes.

She smiled and gave me a pat on the back. Delaney got up and said follow me. I stood there for a while. He stopped and looked at me. I asked him. Where are you going? He replied. Do you want your diamond or not? I looked to the mansion, but he walked toward the horses stable. The insurance woman hold my arm and looked at me. I said okay wait here. So, I went with Delaney. Trust me this was the longest walk I have ever made. I stopped and looked at the insurance women then proceeded. Harm done already nothing to lose. He opened the stable door and a horse instantly neighed. He said wait. He pushed horseshit aside and retrieved a small box. See I told you no one will touch or even steal it. I opened the small box and the smell of horseshit hits my nose first. I said what the fuck. He replied. Like I said no one would even recognize it that it's a diamond. He had covered my precious diamond with cow-dung. It was unrecognizable. The insurance lady just entered when I was holding what looked like cow-dung in my hand. What's that she asked closing her nose. Instantly I retrieved my white handkerchief and started polishing the diamond. There and then I realized that there are two kinds of people in this world. Ones that I have to destroyed and the others that needed to be fostered."

They all stood up and started clapping hands.

"I want everyone here to know that Delaney was the first but not the last. We should all work together to advance humanity. Any acts of sabotage we will be very swift to deal with them."

The Vice President David stood up and walked toward the President Hudson in front of the conference hall. He whispered something in his ears before walking back to sit down. Hudson stopped and looked at everyone. He looked at Kayden for a while before looking at David.

"Are there still enemies among us?"

He walked in front looking at everyone in turn.

"I want to know that I can trust you. I want to believe you have the same goals as us and you will work with us to achieve our goals."

He stopped and looked at everyone. They all got up and started clapping hands for Hudson.

"TWO victory! TWO victory! Our Future! Our Say!"

Nash walked to the corner of a building and removed her sun glasses. She scanned the area before walking back. She instantly stopped and retrieved a gun and turned quickly aiming at a man on top of one of the buildings. The man instantly gestured back, and she lowered the hand holding the gun before proceeding. The man took binoculars and looked everywhere scanning the area. She instantly looked back to the area he had just scanned. He noticed another man taking cover. He whispered something on the two-way radio. A crackling voice startled him. He took his position. A woman instantly appeared from nowhere and walked to the parliament building. She stopped and looked at her chest. She instantly panicked and traced the trajectory red line. Instantly a flash-light blinded her, and she instantly covered her eyes before running inside. Hudson looked at David and relaxed.

Nash looked at a building across the road, then toward another and another before looking ahead of her. She instantly posed and checked her wrist watch. She got in the position and waited. A finger instantly slid inside the trigger circle and the man looked through the lens of the gun and squinted his eye. A man smartly dressed walked very fast wearing an expensive suit. The man on top of the building removed his finger from the trigger circle and took the binoculars and scanned the area. He instantly radioed the others.

"Can someone confirm that that's our target? Where is the motorcade?"

A crackling voice startled him.

"Abort! I repeat Abort! Not subject."

The man relaxed and lowered the gun. The woman carefully looked at the image on her wrist watch and looked at the man walking toward the building.

A crackling voice startled the man on top of the building.

"What is it? Go ahead, I am listening."

There was silence. The woman gazed at the man walking toward her.

Inside David and Hudson were sitting in the office.

"Are you sure we got our man?"

"Yes Sir. Delaney's puppet. Even though he is not aware that he has been tampered with Delaney being Delaney I suggest that we must not take chances. He might be a risk. We don't know what watermarks he has."

"Are you sure?"

"What other option do we have? We deal with him according to protocol."

David looked relaxed. He breathed heavily and looked outside the window.

"Soon it will be all over. A new start total wipe out. We don't want any surprises in the future you know."

"I agree with you Mr. Vice President."

A beep went off startling the two men. David quickly retrieved his pager and looked at it.

"I think he is here."

He radioed. Instantly a beep went off.

David took out his pager and looked at it. Instantly a crackling sound startled him.

"Yes, go ahead."

"It's the subject. Confirm?"

Another beep went off, but this time was from Hudson's laptop. He looked at David, but David gave him a quick glance before walking toward the window. He flipped the curtain and looked outside. Hudson quickly checked the message.

'The beginning 22.'

"The beginning 22." whispered Hudson looking at the laptop.

"What is it Hudson?"

Hudson looked lost in thoughts.

"What is the beginning 22?"

"Hold on," said David walking toward Hudson. Hudson instantly stood up and walked slowly toward the window. He flipped open the curtain and gazed outside. A crackling voice was heard by David.

"Okay……. just hold on," replied David looking at the laptop.

"The beginning 22……?"

He quickly typed something.

Hudson instantly opened the door to go out. David looked at the computer screen.

'Genesis 22' and other options were instantly displayed. He clicked on Genesis 22.

It read;

22 Sometime later God tested Abraham. He said to him,

"Abraham!"

"Here I am," he replied.

2 *Then God said, "Take your son, your only son, whom you love—Isaac—*................ Sacrifice him there as a burnt offering on a mountain *I will show you."*

[New International Version Bible]

Instantly Hudson shouted.

"No! No!"

Instantly David heard gunshots one after the other.

"Hudson!" shouted David getting up and running toward Hudson. He grabbed him and stopped him.

"What are you doing?"

"Let me go right now! Let me go."

He struggled but instantly heard more gunshots. He stopped and looked in horror. The man jerked as bullets riddle his head. Hudson struggled to free himself from David's grip and he elbowed David in the ribs and ran toward the man who was being shot like a dog.

"Don't shoot! Don't shoot!" shouted David.

Hudson screamed and cried profusely running toward the scene. The man fell instantly like a lifeless log. Instantly blood oozed out from his head. Hudson still crying and screaming arrived and threw himself next to the man before holding him in his hands. He looked at him. His face was now unrecognizable with blood oozing from the bullet holes all over.

"His is my son! His is my son! Why!" cried Hudson.

He cried louder and louder holding the man in his hands. Mucus and saliva trickled down his face with every cry.

CHAPTER FIFTEEN

A huge door opened, and a man walked slowly toward a man sat in a seat swinging back and forth.

"Hudson!"

He stopped and looked at the man in front of him.

"Mr. President."

There was no answer. Mr. Vice President David walked toward Hudson and pulled the chair before sitting next to him. He touched his shoulder. The two men sat there in silence. After a while Hudson spoke.

"Did he kill his son?"

"Abraham?"

"Yes. Did he kill his son?"

The Vice President did not answer straight away.

"Delaney must have planned this in advance before he died."

"Answer me damn it. Did this Abraham kill his son?"

"No. Sir."

"So why my son died? Why my boy? Who invited him

here?"

David did not reply.

"Answer me damn it."

"I don't know Sir. I did not even know you had a son. I just tracked the suspect using Delaney's computer and invited him. I thought it was..."

"Damn Mr. Vice President you should have checked. You held me. Why?"

There was a moment of silence. Hudson got up and pushed the swinging chair he was sitting on aside.

"That was my boy. He had nothing to do with this at all. Why kill him. Maybe I put you out of your misery too."

Hudson instantly pulled a gun.

"That was my boy. My fresh and blood. He is not a politician."

The Vice President remained quiet.

"Makes no sense. In that passage it is written that he did not sacrifice his son. This God stopped him. I don't understand why my son had to die. Delaney is dead."

"I apologize, sir."

Hudson punched David very hard that he fell with his chair.

"I truly apologize."

"I can still see my son's blood in my own hands. I can't sleep. Sometimes I wish they had shot me and spared my boy."

David lifted the chair and sat down.

"Delaney was a very bad man an enemy of mankind. Perfectly fitting."

"I don't regret killing that bastard. Why my son? I just sit here and look outside. Somehow, I just wish he could walk in through that door. Who is this Abraham?"

"I can't say for sure."

"Do you think that if this God hadn't had stopped him, he was going to sacrifice his son?"

David remained silent.

"Do you know how hard it is for your son to die first?"

"No Sir."

There was a moment of silence.

"I think this bible is not real. I think it was a colonization manual."

"What are you suggesting? That a man wrote this book? All these stories are lies?"

"I believe so Sir. Looking at the time it was written. It was written at the peak of the 'discovery period.' The colonization period if you like. That time the colonial masters wanted to colonize as much land as possible with little or no resistance and to maintain the colonies in peace."

"Are you sure?"

"Just my opinion. The bible has two meanings. One that's obvious to everyone. A book of stories that happened a long time ago. But to those the bible was written for a powerful manipulating too. A manual of how to do it. To them it is actually telling them what to do."

"Since your son died, I have found out that Delaney or whoever is still doing it targeted the rich."

"Do you mean like a scam?"

"Yes Sir. I have a list here of people in the same situation as you."

"What are you saying? I was targeted?"

"I am afraid yes Sir. I think there are powerful organizations out there that practices what is in the bible. But not the way we know. All these people were misrepresented and tricked into being hacked. That seems like the first stage. This mainly happens to your kids when they are young when you are unlucky to travel to their country or their subsidiaries."

"Okay, I am listening."

"All your wealth will automatically become theirs that is accounted for in their accounting books."

"I don't understand."

"Once you visit their country automatically, they add your wealth to their value of the country and expect you to live there forever."

"What if I want to leave?"

"As long as you leave the money that's no problem."

"If I don't,"

"They don't target you but your son."

"Genesis 22,"

"Exactly. When you stay there, they might just let you keep the money just like keeping it for them."

"But that will be my money."

"I know Sir. They will have added the money to the wealth of their country. So, surveillance and spying becomes the norm. For most they hack the kids when they are young recording everything and listening to all their conversations."

"Is that legal?"

"They have perfected the methods over the years. For most you won't even know it."

"Kayden?"

"Yes Sir. But worse…"

He paused. Hudson looked at him.

"In other countries they tip the secret services and say that you are their spies."

"My son. Are you suggesting that that's what

happened with my son?"

"Yes Sir. I had a tip that there is a spy and all they said was true. I didn't know it was a set up I thought good intelligence."

"Still makes no sense. Why not kill me the owner of the money?"

"You will die quicker than your son in theory but above all..."

"Genesis 22. Obedience?"

"Precisely, Sir."

"But I don't even know this son of a bitch?"

"Abraham never saw God, yet he was prepared to kill his son for him. Power of belief, trust and honor,"

"Is this a game or what?"

"Makes no sense but it is a matter of fact."

"Who else went through this?"

David breathed heavily.

"Olivia, net worth $20billion received a Genesis 22 message just before she witnessed death of her son. She was left traumatized by the incident that she never recovered and died years later."

"Did she leave the money?"

"No but her son was investing $millions abroad. I guess they didn't like that very much. That could explain the early deaths."

The President Mr. Hudson breathed heavily.

"Noel, net worth $600 million. Received the Genesis 22 message before he witnessed horror when his son died in front of him. Still alive but declared unable to manage his finances because of witnessing such a trauma."

The President Hudson kept quiet.

"Mr. Rickson net worth $10 billion witnessed the death of a son. Shot dead by muggers in front of him. Still alive but had several operations including a heart transplant. In and out of the hospital. Bed ridden."

"In all cases the children dies first?"

"Yes Sir. I will explain after, the purpose of all this. Blakely net worth $30 billion. Son and grandson both dead. Received a Genesis 22 message before dying of a heart attack."

"Can't just be Delaney?"

"Organized criminal network that use the bible and other tricks to select and kill off-springs first. Making sure that no one will make claims to the fortune. There is a saying that everything in the world belongs to this 'God'. People are viewed as keeping all this money for him?"

"If not Delaney then who?"

"Zack net worth, $100 million. Received the message and instantly reacted. Offered his son instantly."

"Was his son spared?"

"Yes, but he gave up everything and his son is declared unfit to manage any finances,"

The President stood up, and a tear run down one of his eyes. David paused and looked at him.

"I could have given up everything for him. I was planning to go and spend time with him after all this. All these years I left him with his mum."

He walked to the window and looked outside.

"Miriam, net worth $200 million, received a Genesis 22 message. Daughter killed in front of her. Retired soon after."

"I still don't believe you. Are you saying that they target all these people Mr. Vice President?"

"I would like to believe so. All these are powerful people. People with roles that affect the course of events. We have CEOs of companies, we have attorney generals, we have Presidents, we have managers and law makers."

"So?"

"The main idea is to render one weak and presumed insane?"

"I don't understand."

"These people are power hungry. Take the attorney general for example. If one of them is facing a trial, they influence the outcome. Taking the attorney general for example. If his son died, and he witnessed such a death. If he sits over an important case one might argue that witnessing such a traumatic event can make him incompetent to rule in a case of that importance. Personal circumstances might make him weak and unable to pass tough sentences or give a reasonable judgment. That can be used to overturn a case. The judgment or his decision can be successfully challenged in a court of law. He might suddenly become hesitate just because he witnessed a traumatic event of someone very close to him. He could easily be declared temporary insane just because he witnessed such an event."

The Vice President walked toward the window and stood next to the President.

CHAPTER SIXTEEN

A motorcade of SUVs arrived outside a huge building in the city. The President Mr. Hudson opened the door and looked at the cheering crowd before entering inside. A lot of people were waiting for him. The usher opened the huge doors.

"The honorable Mr. President Hudson!"

"Thank you be seated," shouted the President.

"We are gathered here today to hear the final judgment in the case of Kayden v the global party TWO.

There was complete silence.

"It's with regret that I pass this judgment. It hasn't been an easy road. The events of the last months has left many shaken but..."

The President paused and looked at everyone.

"We must stay focused stay on-course. Change does not come easily. We have a huge task to preserve humanity not just a group of people. Having said that, we must take serious action also against those who will try to reverse previous achievements. We have a moral duty to advance humanity. The *Jus Cogens* laws are laws that any derogation is not permitted and as such these laws have universal jurisdiction that means there can be a collective passing of judgment. In the case of Mr. President Kayden..."

He paused.

"It is with regret that we have found him guilty of misrepresentation. According to protocol he is nothing than a spy."

He paused as there was a huge buzz.

"As such he shall die by firing in public."

Kayden and Paige stood up.

"Your honor with all due respect I think the decision is flawed for the reason that will be clearer soon."

The President did not expect that. This is the first time as far as he can remember when someone challenged his authority and judgment.

"With all due respect I think the President is in no position to pass a judgment that is binding. One that should be recognized by the court."

There was a huge buzz.

"The President fumed with rage.

"Don't waste our time making this drama here. We have important things to do."

"Objection your honor. I will challenge that decision."

The President stood up.

"Challenge all you like but the decision remains unchanged."

"Ladies and gentlemen. What happen to me is something that should not happen to anyone. I suffered after being tricked and misrepresented. I took all corrective steps available to me and sought redress. We were unfortunate because this is a story that need a lot to able to convince anyone. I lost all my fortune. I lost my heart too."

He opened his chest and showed everyone his chest scar.

"It will be unfair after all this pain to suffer further. I have listened to the President, but I think there are other strong grounds that it's unfair and inhumane to do this to me."

"We have laws to follows. Everyone knows that, and everyone follows these laws why not you?"

"I would like to say that the President after witnessing the death of his son. I argue that such a traumatic event especially the fact that it was his son renders him incapable of making a sound judgment. Trauma can be manifested differently in each one of us but nevertheless can render a sound mind to be regarded as temporarily insane. Such a traumatic event will make it impossible for anyone to make sound...."

The President stood up and pulled out his gun.

"Huh!" screamed the people.

Kayden looked at Hudson.

"You shot me?" he whispered.

"Learn to differentiate the two. I am upset but not insane. Comprehend?

David walked and sat next to the President. There was a moment of silence. David looked ahead of him.

"Beautiful weather today."

Hudson remained silent.

"It's your son isn't it?"

"What. Oh yes."

"It happens Sir. These things do really happen, but the big challenge is what you do after such an event. Do you give up? Or you recover quickly because life goes on."

"You are right."

There was silence.

"The idea behind all these Genesis 22 tricks is to render one incompetent therefore unable to make decisions. If you can't make decisions, then you can't be able to run your finances."

"Still Mr. Vice President it does not make any sense. I think there is more to it than what you are saying."

"I was coming to that."

The President threw a quick glance at the Vice President.

"It is a matter of fact that the most profitable businesses are illegal business. Drug trafficking, arms dealers, human trafficking, etc. These people commit evil acts. They are still practicing acts declared inhumane."

"Genocide?"

"Yes, disguised and concealed. All the hacking and torture are all illegal. They bribe everyone involved."

"How do they get away with such evil acts?"

"Bible."

"Bible?"

"Yes, Sir and laws they used to supplement their goals?"

"Is it a fact or just speculation?"

"Take Genesis 22 for example classic example."

"I am listening."

"It reads:

Sometime later God tested Abraham. He said to him, "Abraham!"
"Here I am," he replied.

2 Then God said, "Take your son, your only son, whom you love—Isaac—............... Sacrifice him there as a burnt offering on a mountain *I will show you."*

3 Early the next morning Abraham got up and loaded his donkey. He took with him two of his servants and his son Isaac. When he had cut enough wood for the burnt offering, *he set out for the place God had told him about. 4 On the third day Abraham looked up and saw the place in the distance. 5 He said to his servants, "Stay here with the donkey while I and the boy go over there. We will worship and then we will come back to you."*

6 Abraham took the wood for the burnt offering and placed it on his son Isaac, and he himself carried the fire and the knife. As the two of them went on together, 7 Isaac spoke up and said to his father Abraham, "Father?"

"Yes, my son?" Abraham replied.

"The fire and wood are here," Isaac said, "but where is the lamb for the burnt offering?"

8 Abraham answered, "God himself will provide the lamb for the burnt offering, my son." *And the two of them went on together.*

9 When they reached the place God had told him about, Abraham built an altar there and arranged the wood on it. *He bound his son Isaac and laid him on the altar, on top of the wood. 10 Then he reached out his hand and took the knife to slay his son. 11 But the angel of the Lord called out to him from heaven, "Abraham! Abraham!"*

"Here I am," he replied.

12 "Do not lay a hand on the boy," he said. 'Do not do anything to him. Now I know that you fear God, because you have not withheld from me your son, your only son."

13 Abraham looked up and there in a thicket he saw a ram.... caught by its horns. He went over and took the ram and sacrificed it as a burnt offering *instead of his son. 14 So Abraham called that place The Lord Will Provide. And to this day it is said, 'On the mountain of the Lord it will be provided."*

15 The angel of the Lord called to Abraham from heaven a second time 16 and said, "I swear by myself, declares the Lord, that because you have done this and have not withheld your son, your only son, 17 I will surely bless you and make your descendants as numerous as the stars in the sky and as the sand on the seashore. Your descendants will take possession of the cities of their enemies, 18 *and through your offspring.... all nations on earth will be blessed* [c] *because you have obeyed me."*

[New International Version Bible]

To the ordinary person this is just a bible event that happened a long time ago. To those who the bible was written for it's a manual. A plan to execute a plan. This authorizes one;

first to reduce wood for burnt offerings- this can refer to people on the welfare system or people who can die for life insurance companies to release money in the economy increasing disposable income.

Second passage reads;

"The fire and wood are here," Isaac said, *"but where is the lamb for the burnt offering?"*

Once you have identified the fire and the wood like I said the people who can be killed to release life insurance money or reduce the state welfare system, you will need a lamp. Mind you Mr. President a lamb in Christian circles means a sheep or a gentle, pure, and innocent person. This bible manual states that after identifying the 'wood-people' you will need someone who is innocent, who will die to cover up. His son asked where do we get this lamb, this person to sacrifice who is pure, innocent and gentle? Abraham answered. *God himself will provide the lamb for the burnt offering, my son.*

"I never thought it that way," said the President.

"It gets better. Like I said the bible has two meaning and two purpose. As a manual for the evil and to recruit the lamb to be sacrificed. Those who believe in the bible automatically becomes the lamb to be sacrificed. These people are taught to fight evil. To stand up to evil. To defend their way of life at the same time falling into the lamb-trap. These people will fight after the 'wood' people have been killed. They see this as injustice and therefore will fight. This makes them easy targets. So, in fact the bible [God] has already provided the lamb for a burnt offering."

"I never heard this interpretation before." quipped the President.

"It was not by chance that we managed to destroy Delaney. I was trained since birth Mr. President."

"Ok continue I am listening," said the President.

"The passage goes on to say; *'Abraham built an altar there and arranged the wood on it.'* Having executed his plan, all 'wood' are burnt. To cover his acts and gain the people's support and allegiances, Abraham must build an altar, a shrine or a memorial to connect people with and name all those who died there. This is common practice. The passage went on to say that; *Abraham looked up and there in a thicket he saw a ram... caught by its horns.* Mind you we already have a lamb provided by God [the bible]. This person is innocent and pure, and instincts will kick in after that he attacks the real people behind these atrocities. In turn they set up on him but scared of his life. He runs into hidden. To succeed the culprit-Abraham in this case diverts attention from the 'wood' he killed now to the manhunt. He uses all resources in the search. But this lamb-the innocent person one day he is caught hiding.

The passage continues; *He went over and took the ram and sacrificed it as a burnt offering.* Once the 'lamb or innocent person' is caught Abraham or the evil dictator takes him and sacrificed him to give those with relatives who died some comfort."

"So why kill all these people," asked the President.

"To answer you, I quote the same passage; *Your descendants will take possession of the cities of their enemies.* This is the price. All their wealth will be yours. All their possessions will be yours. This passage is the main drive for all these sacrifices. The relatives of all those who died will be entitled to the life insurance money. A flow of money transfer into the economy."

"But in that passage, you said Abraham did not kill his son. Why then do they kill all their enemies' sons and daughters?" asked the President.

"Any one in power who need to address the economy can use this bible passage to solve that. He can supplement any laws ever heard of the *No Child Left Behind Act?*"

"You mean the law that provides extra money for education of the poor?" asked the President.

"If used with this passage in Genesis 22, It will mean elimination of the child also of the lamb, so no one makes claims to the possession of the lamb that will end up as state possession."

"Can you justify your assumptions?"

"Do you know on 11 September 1853 the first electrical telegraph was used? This rendered the Telegraph Hill obsolete overnight. This is because the Telegraph Hill was used as the first source of information about the cargo that was coming through the Golden gate. This meant knowing and having knowledge of the goods that were on the ships and the lower prices of the commodities. Plenty of goods means lower prices of that good. Shortages means high prices. This information was vital to wholesalers, financiers and merchants. So, this hill was very vital as a source of firsthand information. But the use of the electric telegraph rendered the Telegraph Hill and its twin place the Point Lobos obsolete."

"That sounds very familiar,"

"Precisely Sir. If you look at the Telegraph Hill and imagine Point Lobos next to it what do you have?"

"The World trade center. The twin towers and building 7."

"So, the use of the first electric telegraph on 11 September 1853 hinted on the idea of electronic money. The electronic transfer of money. Just like the adoption of the electric telegraph rendered the

Telegraph hill and its twin Point Lobos obsolete. The electronic money transfer rendered the twin towers obsolete. Here comes Genesis 22 from the bible again. In order to adopt the new electronic system, we must destroy the old system completely. There must be a crush of the system of some kind that will justify the immediate need for the new system. Crushing of the system means destruction of all records and as such will pave way for a new system. No need for paperwork everything will now be accounted electronically. This made in theory the twin towers obsolete."

"But why not exchange all that [the brick, mortar and steel] with a simple electronic money transfer that can mean funds transfers, insurance transfer, compensation transfer, etc.?"

"We have the plan the solution but how are we going to achieve that?"

"Why not flash-out our lamb? Remember the bible Genesis 22 said God will provide the lamb. God advised Abraham to go and sacrifice."

"So, a missile in June 2001 kills twenty-three. Ball rolling in play in the hope that they will send bigger missiles too."

"Retaliation."

"Obviously the enemies will aim for the symbolic ornaments but also not knowing they are just being coached to do what the master-minder want them to do."

"I don't believe you."

"Just like with the bible. A means to an end for the lamb."

"The lamb will retaliate send in revengeful man. Back to Genesis 22. Fulfill all the highlighted factors. Locate the mountain. Twin Towers. Cut wood for a burnt offering. All paper documents about trading, all records in physical forms should be set on fire to pave way for the new system that can only be justified after destruction of old system. Then look for the lamb God provided. Here comes Sabila. The Twin Towers are rendered obsolete flattened to ground level by plane crushes. Then build an altar or a shrine with the names of all those who perish. That releases life insurance money to the remaining relatives. That releases compensation money transfers. The people are hurt they need some comfort and resolve over this. Then find the lamb on the run and in hiding. Send your men to get him and once caught offer him as a burnt offering too."

"You are just speculating. How do the one in power defend all this,"?

"The President shouted; 'sabotage'. How can I defend what is rightfully mine from sabotage-attacks? He asked. Did you see he nearly killed me too? Have you ever heard of the term self-defense people? No matter what I do this guy is always on the attack, sabotaging everything. I must defend myself and our way of life. The President's building somehow was hit by a plane and suffered damage. Sabila's compound was hit by an Apache helicopter. The lamb in this case Sabila is captured, but the bible says spare your son and sacrifice this lamb because he is pure and innocent."

The President looked at the Vice President.

"*In Leviticus 1v10 it reads; If the offering is a burnt offering from the flock, from either the sheep or the goats, you are to offer a male without defect. 11 You are to slaughter it...* Straight away we can see that the person blamed and to be killed is technically pure and flawless otherwise God would not accept the offering."

"But Mr. Vice President in Genesis 22 it does not say you must sacrifice the son of the lamb. But they killed Sabila's son as well?"

"Here comes a new law to take into account just that; No Child Left Behind Act passed into law in 2001 after the twin towers were rendered obsolete. The same passage concludes that *your descendants will take possession of the cities of the enemies.* That can also explain and justifies the No Child Left Behind Act. If you are to take the possessions no one shall challenge rights to that property. Looking at Sabila's father he was worth $20 billion. How then do we possess all the assets as ordered by Genesis 22? They passed as law the Terrorists Assets Freezing and Confiscating Acts."

"Convincing, but I am the President and can't accept your assumptions."

"You must believe me. These are manuals on how to rob in day light and solve all your problems. A governing tool for the Presidents would you think so?"

"Don't make me laugh. Just a coincidence."

The two men laughed.

THE END

Carolinadeivid